For Blade "Everglades" Shamade.
We all knew that wasn't your real name, but you were a stubborn bastard and I admire that.

Contents

Never Self-Publish a Book

Cool, look at this website!
Won't I get arrested for that?
No not that one, this one. It says I can self-publish my own book!
Oh right, because I really think you should close down that other website immediately.
I could be a real author.
And never open it again.
I could be rich and famous.
Still open.
Oh for goodness sake! There, it's gone.
Anyway, isn't self-publishing just for people who can't get their work sold by real publishers because they're not very good at writing?
Oh how wrong you are. This is a great platform for budding new writers to get their work out there.
Oh, OK then.
I'm going to be a celebrity. I'm going to buy a mansion in LA. I'm going to take over the world!
Alright, calm down.
Don't tell me to calm down. You can't tell people what to do.
I'm not really telling you what to do, I'm just suggesting that you relax a little and...
You wouldn't like it if I told you to get out of your own home.
You do that all the time!
You're imagining things. Now fetch me a fine herbal tea and my writing spectacles.
Why would I do that?
Why does anyone do anything? Why am I sniffing this bag of toenail clippings?

Those aren't sufficient answers.
Sniffs
How long have you been collecting those?
It's not important.
Well it is a bit weird, I mean...
Quiet now. It's time to create my masterpiece. Leave me be.
But you're in my house.
I said leave me!
You're a very odd person and I don't know why we're friends.

The above dialogue is one that could have happened in any ordinary homestead, bowling green or site of ritual human sacrifice. Perhaps the first character had searched for years for a way to express himself. Maybe he was tired of a dull life; one filled with long hours in an office or endless chores at home. Maybe both of these people had great aspirations and dreams that were yet to be realised. Maybe those dreams were the only things that got them out of bed in the morning. Maybe they didn't have beds. Maybe they had several. One of those beds may have resembled a shoe; another like a fox eating vomit. Maybe they didn't like musicals. Or maybe they did. Perhaps they didn't believe in cabbage. We will never know and it's not important. Although, thinking about it now, they probably did believe in cabbage. Most people do.

The subject they were discussing is more significant. The notion of self-publishing a book. The effortless, low intensity path towards having something on the bookshelf with your name on it. That seems pretty cool, right?

Wrong. Self-publishing wont bring you any respect, fame or fortune. People wont think you're cool. If you want respect then go do something that's actually impressive; like volunteering at a homeless shelter or negotiating your way into a colony of alien bees and overpowering their queen.

The identity of the world's first self-published book is a hotly debated subject. Many believe Gregory Yanooth's somewhat confusing treatise about desks was the original. Entitled *Is it a Desk?*, on every page it asked the question "Is it a desk?" next to a picture of an object. The answer was invariably "Yes, it is a desk". The picture was almost never a desk. A silly book, to say the least.

Yanooth spent most of his life in abject poverty, making little hats for finger puppets which nobody ever bought- much like his book. He was probably the first, but certainly not the last, victim of the self-publishing lie.

Don't fall into the trap. Don't rush into this venture thinking that the process will be like the exciting creation of the world's greatest barn museum, when in fact it will turn out more like a yarn museum. Feel free to switch the order of those similes if you prefer yarn to barns… you sad loser! Barns are way better. They have doors! Does yarn have doors? No. I rest my case!

The excitement felt in the planning stage will turn to anger and shame when the finished book is inevitably less interesting than a man who gets excited by things just because they have doors. Maybe leave it to the professionals. Or, by all means try to write and rewrite your story before sending it to proper editors and actual publishers who know what they're doing. Most likely you'll fail miserably and have to rethink your life, but that's fine. Not everyone is a creative genius. However, while we're on that subject let's take a look at some actual best sellers and see what *does* make a good book.

Laura's Having a Laugh tells the story of male stripper Laura Kezz, who started laughing at a cookery program and didn't stop until he was bludgeoned to death by gorillas forty seven years later. This text took many decades to craft and the hard work has clearly paid off. It is rightfully regarded as one of the best books about a male stripper, called Laura Kezz, who started laughing at a cookery program and didn't stop until he was bludgeoned to death by gorillas forty seven years later, that has ever been told.

Or who could forget that memorable quote that will last throughout the ages, from Henton B Quenton's *Life Love Death and Sheds*.

> "It takes more than one man to build a shed. Unless that one man is skilled in the ways of shed making, or it is simply an easy shed to assemble."

So powerful.

So, to recap, self-published books do not go through the same rigorous editing and scrutiny of genuine books. The quality of writing is sub standard, and the creators are generally uninteresting and rarely held in the same high regard as traditional authors, actors or erotic lampshade vendors. Also, self-publishing can, possibly, lead to the writer growing an extra nose covered in big puss filled boils and crusty scars. Most likely the writer will become shunned in his or her own community; called names like Two Nose Jones, Boily Boily

Bastard or Timothy. There are almost no detailed documented cases of this not happening.

***

Pete.
Yes?
I'm pregnant.
Ah.
Ah? That's all you have to say?
Ah mazing.
That's better.
I'm glad I covered that up or she might have got mad with me.
Pete, you just said that out loud.
Oh no, I think I said that out loud.
Yes you did. You're still talking out loud.
Perhaps I should change the subject quickly.
I can hear you, you idiot!
Look Jane, a natterjack toad.
Oh really? I love natterjack toads.
Ha. She fell for it. Dumb, ugly, pathetic Jane.
That's the last straw. I can't believe you would lie about the presence of a natterjack toad! Goodbye forever Pete!

One might wonder why Jane- when she clearly heard Pete call her dumb and pathetic- would focus on the lack of natterjack toads rather than the insult. This is because natterjack toads are awesome. They can travel on water and fly long distances providing the most useful form of transportation for many residents of the Alaskan bush. Oh no, actually that's seaplanes not natterjack toads.

Anyway, the point of this little dialogue is to depict unrest and deep feelings of resentment and loathing as they come to a boiling point. Many people like to vent their anger through writing and numerous books allow erudite thinkers and philosophers to get across their ideas to a wide audience. On the flip side of this, self-published works allow boring, unimportant nobodies to also have their say. Luckily no one will ever buy or read their books.

Why do these people believe that anyone cares what they think? Their life story? Don't care. Their political views? Yawn. Endless, whining rants with vulgar language and poorly argued points? No thanks. Nobody gives a damn!

However, if I did want to rant I *could* complain about quite a few things. For example; in my perfect world those who pretend to like the taste of beer (when we all know alcohol is solely a means to a drunken end) would have their thoughts reprogramed in a nice, comfortable re-education camp.

And people who stand two abreast on escalators blocking the path for everyone else. Have you no heart? Does the thought of anyone else apart from you and your slow, lazy accomplice ever enter your selfish selfish mind? Dead! You'd be dead first!

And people who put on a movie and then proceed to talk over it. Are you fucking insane!? Why would you agree to watch something and then speak over it? Or worse, watch some awful ten second video clips on your phone, at full volume, distracting yourself and others from the film you have already agreed to view? Inexcusable! What's the point of putting it on in the first place? How do you hope to know what's going on in the story or the facts of the documentary? Oh that's right you don't. You'll just ask me hundreds of questions when you stop blathering on for two seconds or you peek up for a sanity break from your obnoxious phone videos.

It's the whole constant need to be socialising thing that bothers me. Like the absolute time wasting filth who show up to pub quizzes to chat and mess about. No! Get out of my team and remove yourself from my table, sir. I am in a prearranged group of adequate numbers. I don't need you "popping in" *late* and offering no attempt whatsoever at an answer. I'd rather you didn't disrupt the team by talking about work, or your terminally ill spouse, or some other inapt drivel that does not belong in a conquest of learned minds.

When someone goes online to tell the world *I'm so bored* I feel like setting their house on fire. Maybe that would add some excitement to the crap life of the unimaginative twat.

I also hate stupidly large lawns. And what about plastic forks? Am I right? They're really shit aren't they? Don't you agree?

But like I say, I don't like reading people's angry rants and I would never waste time writing such self important garbage myself.

***

Basically, in conclusion, self-publishing can lead to great disappointment. Like the disappointment one might feel when they lose their favorite ironing board cover or get beaten in a game of Tic-tac-toe by a sentient saucepan. Or like when you rush to publish a book of short stories with a whimsical name like… I don't know… *Ballad's Breasts and Beans for Feet.* Later you realise it's full of spelling mistakes and cemented with sub parr stories that you hurriedly typed up in order to add to the pathetic page count. Or the disappointment felt when you ask your friends David and Simon to add to your new book and they write far more interesting and funny texts than your own.

But you'll probably not listen to me will you? I've said all I care to on the subject and I suppose you'll do as you please despite my reservations. Much like my friend Craig Yifter who enjoys throwing postage stamps. They never get very far because they're virtually weightless but this doesn't stop him.

"Why are you throwing stamps?" The people yell.
"You're an idiot." They say
"You'll never amount to anything, you smelly wanker!" cries his mum.

Yet this doesn't deter him. He's a real trooper.
In truth his dedication to a pointless and frankly ridiculous hobby inspires me to carry on living in this often pointless and ridiculous world.

To conclude this conclusion, collecting toenails in a bag and sniffing them is frowned upon. Natterjack toads are great. Always take care of your ironing board covers. And never self-publish a book!

CROCINO

"It's back!" cried Douglas, sweat dripping from his brow. "The creature lives!"

John Hazeltrout woke himself from his pleasant dreams about goats that made exceedingly good nut roasts and sat upright.

"Are you sure?"

"One hundred percent!"

How could this be? John had surely killed his creation three years ago, hadn't he?

"Has it killed yet?"

Douglas frowned. "I don't think so. I mean I don't really know. Oh, I'm sorry John but as soon as I saw it I came running back to your bathroom."

John needed to know everything.

"So you definitely saw the creature?"

"Yes. Then I ran here and I had to use your toilet."

"Tell me every detail!"

Douglas raised his eyebrows. "Well, I noticed a long watery brown skid mark so I knew that you weren't too fussed on toilet hygiene. I thought you wouldn't mind if I relieved my aching bowels so I undid my belt, dropped my trousers and-"

"About the creature, Douglas! Tell me everything you saw it do."

Douglas had seen only a brief glimpse before running away, much like an easily satisfied peeping Tom. John hoped that his friend was mistaken.

"I hope you are mistaken," he said; a logical thing to say considering how he felt.

"Diving board!" said Douglas; an illogical thing to say considering its irrelevance to the situation. John sighed impatiently. He would get nowhere by questioning Douglas. One thousand thoughts swam through his mind. How could the creature still be alive? Would he be able to stop it this time? Why did that one goat with the green beard always add crayons to his nut roasts? Plus nine hundred and ninety-seven other thoughts.

"What are you going to do?" Douglas asked.

"Something I should have done a long time ago!"

"Clean the toilet?"

"What? No, I'm going to kill the creature."

John posed heroically, just long enough for Douglas to look up at him in admiration, before he sprinted as fast as his legs could carry him. His ageing body soon began to tire. His legs felt weak, his body a burden that he could not carry. Still, he ran on. Time ticked by and John ran further, not daring to stop for breath lest his creation gain more time to kill. His body felt heavy like a large fridge, his lungs like two pressure cookers fit to explode and his bladder bulged like an obese woman's waistline. Still John ran. With sweat oozing out of every pore he felt as if he was going nowhere. He *was* going nowhere!

"Maybe you should get off the treadmill John." suggested Douglas.

"Blast!" moaned John. "I should never have put this on the front doorstep."

"Shall we take the car then?"

"Yes Douglas, let's take the car! And bring the shotgun."

When they arrived at the centre of town a horrible sight greeted them, one that turned John's stomach. Two teenagers were holding hands and flirting joyfully; even kissing, in a public place. They were behaving like rapscallions. Or worse-ragamuffins!

Some years previously two of John's closest friends had expressed their love for each other openly. Frequently they would lock tongues without a care in the world about what was going on around them. They certainly didn't take any notice of what their prudish friend John thought. Nor did they take any notice of the speeding cement truck that was heading their way as they kissed with closed eyes. They became forever frozen in that embrace as concrete statues that John occasionally drew funny little moustaches on late at night.

Groaning in disgust John shook an angry fist at the teens.

"Why did you do that?" asked Douglas.

"I know, I probably should have hit them with a blunt instrument but there were none at hand."

"Why don't you like seeing happy couples, John?"

This was an unusually poignant question for his friend to have asked and a lump caught in John's throat as he answered.

"I once loved and lost. She could have been the one. But alas, she moved on and I let fear hold me back from chasing after her."

"That's sad." Said Douglas.

John turned his face away and continued.

"When I visited last and tried to kiss her she politely declined. That ship had sailed."

"You were in love with a *boat*?"

"No, Douglas, it's just a phrase."

"I loved a boat once too."

"I never said I loved a boat, Douglas, do not get the wrong impression here."

"It was quite a small boat; more of a bathtub really…"

But Douglas's romantic ramblings were cut short when the very creature they were tracking appeared from behind a building that looked a bit like a ladle. John would have pondered this strangely shaped building at a less stressful time. He may have thought *what a strange shape? Why would it be shaped like that? I would love some soup. Oh, how I love crusty bread with my soup.*

But right now he ignored the building almost entirely and- after wiping the saliva from his chin that had collected while he was thinking about delicious soup- he saw the beast.

Standing before him was a gigantic crocodile, at least thirty feet long, his creation, a huge scaly reptile more terrifying than any other. John froze like a naked man in the snow, but he wasn't naked. He had remembered to wear clothes since his last fine. Neither was it snowing. John was petrified because this was no ordinary crocodilian. This was Crocino! John's project, his life's work, and his nemesis. The one creature they all said could never live. The crocodile with a rhino's anus!

The oddly shaped monster had dark grey rhino cheeks protruding obscenely from it's back, at the base of its tail. It looked ridiculous and repulsive. Crocino's very appearance brought on a strong feeling of queasiness; like footage of a road accident or your grandmother's face.

Townsfolk were running and screaming all around them.
"It's going to kill us all!"
"Run for your lives!"
"Crocodile!" someone wailed.
"With a rhino's ass!" someone added.

John snapped back to reality and raised the trusty old shotgun that he affectionately called ′Princess Keith′. Crocino roared in anger and, spinning around, he tail-whipped John off his feet. The shotgun sprawled onto the road far out of his reach.

In times of hardship, John had always been the more reliable of the two friends. He would keep calm and overcome any physical or mental challenge while Douglas fell to pieces or broke down hysterically. But this time Douglas held all the cards.

"Why are you holding all those cards?" asked John. "Put them down and come and help me!"

What was the use? Winded and bruised John smiled a maniacal smile. Crocino drew ever closer to him but still he grinned like an insane man at some sort of grinning competition.

"Look at you. My beast! Maybe it's right that you kill me. I am very much like you after all. I mean apart from the rhino anus."

Crocino paused and tilted his head as if he somehow knew what was being said.

"I lost all my scientific credibility when I began working on you. We're both freaks. Neither of us belongs here really. I'm much too intelligent and you're far too dangerous."

Douglas wiped tears from his cheeks as he crawled slowly towards the shotgun.

John continued "Do it Crocino! Finish me!"

All at once Crocino pounced, Douglas grabbed the shotgun and John snatched a grenade from his pink and yellow top-hat. (He was wearing a pink and yellow top-hat; It didn't seem important enough to mention earlier). Douglas shot at Crocino who snapped round to face him as John threw the grenade. It soared above Crocino's head.

"You've missed!" cried Douglas.

"No I haven't."

The grenade sank perfectly between the now very much endangered rhino cheeks and exploded with a loud bang, one last growl and several splat-splat-splats.

"We're safe!" cried the townsfolk.

"Huzzah!" someone cheered.

"They dealt with that crocodile and made it snappy." joked a particularly witty crowd member.

"I'm a filing cabinet!" added a local idiot.

John breathed a sigh of relief. "Come on Douglas. Let's go home."

Back in the comfort of John's living room, the two friends discussed Crocino's history. Then they prank phone-called their mutual friend, Dan, and made rude noises. After they had stopped giggling they discussed Crocino again.

"Of course! We only asked Crocino nicely not to kill anyone. We never actually defeated him before." said John.

"Seems like an odd thing to forget." Douglas mused.

"We must have terrible memories."

"Yeah. Come on let's prank phone call our mutual friend Dan and make rude noises."

And so John and Douglas remained great friends until their untimely deaths of syphilis and a tree felling incident respectively. John never did realise his dream of eating a nut roast made by goats: a privilege that you and I all too often take for granted today.

Dracula: A Most Dreadful Account of a Vampyre, or, The Beast of the Night who Stalks his Prey Through Satanic Means and Hates Garlic and Fails to Take Swift Action

Beware readers for henceforth shall be the terrible and true tale of a tumultuous time of torment and tribulations, tied together by twisting accounts and tantalising titbits. Those of you whom are weak of heart or base in courage should seek no further the truth of the heinous Count Dracula and his diabolically sinister shenanigans, for the terror of knowing that such events truly occurred may shock you to death...and kill you!

For legal reasons I am bound to insert that death while in the possession of this book is not an admission of guilt on the part of the author, the publisher or the vendor.

Therefore, enjoy...or do not…

From the Diary of Jonathon Harker, 3rd May 1890

Dear diary, it is with excitement mixed with trepidation that I write this entry, for today I have entered the lands of Transylvania where excitement and trepidation await me. The humble folk of this land are a grim sort, wearing mostly grey and black, shuffling about like corpses and muttering under their breath in colourless tones. And they're all so ugly.

I arrived this morning by train with my satchel full of papers and a cross about my neck, a gift from my dearest Mina who fears the land of Transylvania to be godless. I laughed in her pretty, naive face and said that I had nothing to fear from the primitive superstitions of simple lands, but alas dear Mina fainted when I mentioned the word 'fear', her womanly sensibilities overcoming her. So I wore the cross to appease her and though she is far, far away I can still feel her touch upon my breast where the cross hangs, though of course she being but my fiancée she has never touched more than the hem of one of my shirt sleeves. We had to apologise to the vicar on that occasion, such was our embarrassment.

At first I struggled to find suitable transportation, my regional Transylvanian being somewhat rusty when compared to my knowledge of French, Spanish, Latin, Mandarin, Swahili and the language of Caribbean Pygmies who eat their young. Eventually, through gesturing and a healthy amount of coin-purse jingling I established a rapport with a coachman and I sat within his hearse-like carriage on the final part of my journey from London, to the seat of Count Dracula, a charming fellow by all accounts.

As I write this the carriage is swaying to and fro upon the ancient dirt roads and boulderdashed pathways of the mountainous region, a grave mistake for my penmanship. I shall therefore return to my diary whence I am arrived at Castle Dracula. So for now I sign off, to return at a later date to fill in further my travels and the no doubt boring and mundane events that will fill my life for the next year. Yes, I depart this particular entry with grace and fulfilment, knowing that I have written down what indeed I have witnessed so far. The final chapter of this opening chapter has come, and so I sign off. For now. For it is indeed the end of my beginnings in Transylvania, this land of trees and mountains and ruinous folk. So fare thee well, I say, you who are reading this. I put my words into your ears through your mind. When next we meet I shall have more to say. But now I must end this entry here.

For though I will likely have much to say in the near future, right now I have reached a happy conclusion to my opening musings. So please come back when...oh, we have arrived.

The carriage has come to a stop in front of a huge looming castle high up in the mountains and there is a tall, thin man in a dark cloak before me. He is beckoning me to get out of the carriage. Now he is beckoning more readily. Now his face has grown a small scowl. He is approaching the door. He is opening it. He is asking me to stop writing. He is asking me to stop reading aloud as I write. He is growing somewhat impatient. He has grabbed my diary and thrown it to the ground, I write lying on the cobbles in the castle courtyard.

From the Diary of Jonathon Harker, 7th May 1890

What a strange fellow this Count Dracula is. Why just the other day he turned into a mist and crept into my bedroom from under the door. Most peculiar.

The odd occurrences began at dinner on the first evening: as I was chewing on a ripe tomato the juice spurted forth from my mouth and spattered the front of my dinner jacket. Naturally I was abysmally embarrassed and apologised profusely, then I attempted to lighten the mood by suggesting that it looked like I was some blood sucking demon who was a messy eater. At that moment I looked up and terror gripped me by the throat: the Count, with his pale skin and permanently bloodshot eyes, was filing his nails at the dinner table. I almost vomited with horror.

The next day the Count came to kiss me good morning and found me at my toilet, shaving. He requested I use the sink instead and so I obliged, not wishing to upset my host. Unfortunately the Count's talking about his taste for human flesh distracted me to the point that I sliced my neck with my razor. A tiny amount of blood seeped out, but the Count lunged at me with vigour in his eyes, clamping his mouth around the wound and sucking fitfully. Then, just as suddenly as it had happened he stopped and withdrew, looking rather apprehensive. I thanked him for attending to my wound so dutifully and continued on my shaving, noting with abject terror that he hadn't washed his hands!

But it was on the third evening that I met the most bizarre instance of the Count's behaviour I have yet to overcome: as I was exploring the castle I happened to peak out of a window at the majestic vistas. I leant out and spied a dark shape leaning out of a window further below. It was the Count. I was about to call out to him when he fell! But instead of plummeting he clung to the side of the castle and began to descend, his shape becoming that of a huge beast with wings. And then he leaped from the side and soared away over the mountains. I was speechless: he didn't even say goodbye.

Are these poor manners or simply odd customs? Either way I must watch my back, there's no telling what sort of folk dance I may be dragged into.

From the Diary of Jonathon Harker, 22nd May 1890

I am a prisoner, and the Count is my warden, and the iron bars at the window are my iron bars at the window. I am trapped here, forced to go only where the Count allows. He leaves in the morning before I rise and doesn't return until late in the evening, and in the meantime though I am free to explore the castle at my leisure I find that my way is often blocked. So many doors, and so many of them beyond my access. Damn these 'please do not enter' signs!

In my desperation to find a way out I even tied some bed sheets together and used them as a rope to climb out of the window, but I inadvertently tied them to the Count himself as an anchor, a fact I only realised when half way down the rope began pulling me back in. When I reached the top I told the Count I was just sightseeing. He did nothing except to open his mouth wide and breathe deeply onto my face. The stench was ungodly, like a rotten guinea pig paw, and I held my nose and said 'pee-ewe!' while waving my hand in front of my face. The Count, unamused, leapt out of the window and turned into the flying beast again, taking the bed sheets with him. He was gone before I could tell him he had a trail of toilet paper caught in the hem of his cloak.

From the Diary of Jonathon Harker, 30th May 1890

Gypsies!

From the Diary of Jonathon Harker, 30th May 1890

Damned gypsies.

From the Diary of Jonathon Harker, 11th June 1890

My sanity is failing me, for surely I have not seen spectres and phantoms else the world that I understand is no more. After a moment of pure unadulterated impoliteness I disregarded a sign on one of the doors and barged my way in with a polite knock to make sure anyone inside were decent.

Within was a dark and musty room covered in cobwebs and dust. And piled up throughout were rectangular wooden boxes, about the height and shape of the Count, and curiously cut into the shape of a coffin. In fact, one might assume they were coffins if not for the fact that I have no good reason to assume that the shape-changing, blood sucking, ill-mannered Count was at all odd.

I opened one to find it full of dirt (pornographic articles and the like) and earth (a globe that one might find in a classroom) and mud (a poster for a theatrical play starring a Matthew McConaughey). But in the second one I found a note saying 'please fill me with soil' and underneath that another note that said 'there's no double meaning here, move along.' I was perplexed: how on Earth did Matthew McConaughey become such a celebrated actor?

I left that room in a daze, and didn't stop wandering until I bumped into one of the Count's maids. I apologised and moved along, only realising when I was halfway down the corridor that the Count didn't have any maids. He cleaned the house from top to bottom by himself, looking rather pretty in a piny as he did so. I turned to see a flowing white silk dress sweep away round the corner so I chased it, but at a polite distance so I didn't look like I was letching.

The woman was tall, thin and pale, just like the Count, and her breasts were voluminous, just like the Count. She seemed to glide over the stones as effortlessly as a fart and I found myself unable to take my gaze off her. At one point she turned coquettishly towards me and bit her lip, drawing blood from her ruby red lips. I thought it mildly flirtatious until she winced and said 'ow, I bit my lip again' and ran off, disappearing through the narrow crack in the edge of a doorframe. I followed, wondering why she bothered with the tiny crack when the door was wide open.

Inside I found the woman with two others, all dressed the same in white silken nightdresses. Their lips were red as blood and their hair was smooth, flowing and lustrous. I thought at that moment they may have been stealing my conditioner. The one I followed there beckoned me over with a pretty finger, twirling her hair with another. The remaining two girls cupped their breasts, kissed each other vigorously and squeezed each others' buttocks. Another odd local custom, I observed with vague and uninterested interest. I swear that nothing but my dearest Mina was on my mind, I swear it my darling.

Suddenly the room and the mood were interrupted by the Count bounding into the room. I pulled my pantaloons up as fast as I could and fled as the Count began berating the girls and brandishing a deflated balloon. Needless to say I was happy to leave that awful place and only returned a handful of times to make sure my observations were accurate.

I love you Mina.

From the Diary of Jonathon Harker, 30th June 1890

I must escape, for I fear my life is in grave danger. While wandering through the castle as I have become accustomed to do the Count accosted me and grabbed me by the throat, pushing me up against a wall as effortlessly as if I were a child. He snarled like an animal and told me that he wished to drain the blood from my veins and turn my empty body into a vessel for his dark machinations, which upset me greatly for I am fond of my blood.

Shaking, I returned to my bedroom and decided to concoct an escape plan. It would have to be daring, cunning and secret, for the Count has spies everywhere, even the wolves and the trees. I have seen them from my window, gathering together. Never has a copse of trees looked more sinister. On one occasion a wolf spotted me staring and drew its paw across its throat. Chilling indeed.

Without bed sheets I could not descend the exterior castle wall, so my only recourse was to walk through the front door and wait at the bus stop. But the carriages were rather costly in this part of the country and I regret I had spent most of my money on the slot machines in the Count's basement. But I have seen travelling minstrels in the local village performing tricks and playing music, and how the village folk cheer and throw coins at their feet. Sometimes the villagers come up to the castle to offer animals to the Count, no doubt so he can put them in a petting zoo for young children to adore. If I can craft a costume for my performance I can play it out for the villagers when they come and gather the money they offer me.

The question then is, how does one craft nipple tassels out of curtains?

From the Log of the Demeter, 6th July 1890

Argh, me hearties. 'tis I, the captain of the Demeter, and what a haul of booty we have on our fine ship. With fine trading sought and curried, we bring upon the ship a cargo of coffin-shaped boxes full of earth that we accepted from a tall, dark stranger on the coast of Transylvania, argh! A madman though he be, he be a wealthy one too. Why, he even paid me to speak and write like a stereotypical pirate while he remains onboard, yarr, to which I be only too happy to oblige for an extra dubloon or two a day.

So me hearties, to England, home of supple virgins as our benefactor do say so himself, yarr!

From the Diary of Dr. Seward, 20th July 1890

I write today with some concern noting the health of one of my longer-interned patients Renfield. Though he resides in the green and pleasant land of England, home of supple virgins, he is beleaguered with a sickness of the mind that renders him sometimes insane yet in his loftier moments he remains a gentleman of impeccable manners and courtesy. This is nothing new, as any interlopers upon my private diary will know (you know who you are, Gregory!) for Renfield has often slipped between his lucid moments and far-fetched blathering. But recently the sickness seems to be taking hold of him to a degree substantially further than ever before.

Let me recall, for the benefit of those reading (Gregory), the instance of today: I was making my usual rounds when I came to Renfield's room, and the sight within shocked me to my core! The sparrows I had allowed him were gone, eaten by their very owner himself!

Ah, but I see I must explain. Let me recall the instance of earlier this week, when I visited Renfield to find him very happy and bright. I noted with surprise that he had gathered a group of sparrows on his windowsill and was very excited that his experiment had worked. 'Yes indeed,' I remarked.

Ah, but I see I must explain further. Let me recall the instance of the previous week, when Renfield told me he was going to perform an experiment to see if he could coax sparrows to his cell.

Anyway, I diverge pointlessly. The fact is that Renfield had eaten them.

I asked him as to why, but he spoke in words I could not comprehend, his mouth being full of sparrow. Once he'd swallowed the one in his mouth he was able to tell me of his visions, of a tall, thin and pale man who was coming here, to England, to spread his corrupting influence. He was calling to Renfield, so I gathered, to join him and become his intern. As terrible as the notion was it was compounded by the revelation that it was to be an unpaid internship. Such diabolical madness is surely beyond the realm of rational thought, and so I must conclude that Renfield has succumbed to a new madness, beyond what he was experiencing previously.

My only comfort in these trying times is the knowledge that dear Lucy Westenra may soon by my wife. She always wanted doves at her wedding, I wonder if Renfield can teach me his trick.

From the Diary of Mina Murray, 24th July 1890

I begin this journal by writing of my intent to keep note of everything that happens for no particular reason, endeavouring to remember, in perfect detail, everything that is said and seen by me and to me. In this way I hope that if any strange and unbelievable events take place I shall have a diary of evidence to look back on to piece it all together.

That being said I have arrived in joyful Whitby by way of carriage. The sun is shining, the ambient temperature is balmy, the wind is mild and I currently count thirteen clouds in the sky. On the way here we passed forty other carriages, a wagon, two rambling peddlers and two-hundred-and-one flies.

Counting so dutifully has reduced my faculties and now I am tired however, so perhaps I shall take slightly less notice of my surroundings. I am sure I will write down just enough to be relevant later on should the need arise.

I find my dear friend Lucy Westenra in a gay mood, and also very happy, to see me after so long apart. She speaks ceaselessly of having received no less than three marriage proposals from a doctor, a Lord's son and an American, all fine occupations indeed. One would think the taxing task of choosing one of them to take her hand would be a blight upon her womanly sensibilities, but she takes it all in her stride, fainting only once or twice a day.

In contrast I myself am wracked with anxiety as to the fate of my dearest Jonathon, whose absent correspondence grows heavily on my mind. When last I heard he was on his way to meet one Count Dracula to discuss legal matters of heirship and such. I do not pretend to understand the complicated world of men, with their 'numbers' and 'words', instead contenting myself with the happy knowledge that I will one day bear my dear Jonathon's children and hire a nanny to look after them while I sew in front of the fireplace.

I pray to God that my beloved Jonathon is safe and chaste, and that if he were not either I would be notified immediately so I could take appropriate action. A large and heavy bible can cure sin in many ways.

From the Diary of Mina Murray, 26th July 1890

Oh joy, what good news I have received! My dearest Jonathon is returned to England and is safe and well, so says his good friend and mentor Mr. Hawkins via letter. As I write this I am simultaneously reading his letter so that I can put down my thoughts as they come, rather than gather them at the end and make a rounded interpretation of the letter for dramatic effect.

He says that Jonathon is handsome (good) with firm buttocks (as I knew him to be) and soft lips (such a relief to know those lips are in safe hands). But see, he then goes on to say that Jonathon is rather subdued and pale, and that he arrived in queer dress, with nipple tassels made out of Transylvanian curtains, though he admits his estimations may be off as his history of curtains is a little rusty.

Mr. Hawkins then writes that upon consultation with a doctor he believes Jonathon to be healthy and of sound mind, save for his babbling of witnessing an aristocratic man display terrible table manners. I laugh thusly: huh, huh, huh, and cover my mouth delicately with a gloved hand. My Jonathon is weary from travel and knows I must be frightfully worried for him, so he lightens the mood with a harmless jest. No such man exists, for if he did he would be pure evil and no such creature exists on God's fair Earth.

I reply in turn, and ask Mr. Hawkins to kiss my sweet Jonathon for me, in the manner that I might once we are married. I know that he'll appreciate the gesture. Now I am writing that I am looking forward to seeing Jonathon in a few days time when he will come to see me. Now I am writing that I am also writing this. And now, that I am writing this. Then this. Now I am writing that I am in a loop and that I am laughing at my silly predicament at not being able to stop writing about writing about about writing about writing about about writing about this.

Thankfully I have run out of paper and so I seal the envelope and am preparing to take it to the post-master's office forthwith. I shall take a guinea with me for the postman, and also a hamster. He says they are a delicacy.

But my joy at hearing news from Jonathon is tempered somewhat by my apprehensions for Lucy, for she has taken to wandering about in the night. Naturally, she being completely healthy with nothing to suggest otherwise, her innocuous and harmless sleepwalking fills me with great concern. I have seen her wandering about the place, even through the door at the front of the house and down through the streets. I followed her on each of these occasions but daren't disturb her, watching silently as she gazed up at the graveyard on the hill, played hopscotch on the cobblestones and ordered a round of drinks at the rowdy inn on the harbour side. Such strange behaviour indeed.

From the Log of the Demeter, 28th July 1890

Shiver me timbers, something strange be afoot! Since the journey from non-strange Transylvania with our non-strange guest and his non-strange coffin-shaped boxes of dirt, the crew be disappearing! Yar! First it be Turkish Tim (the Greek), then No-legs Peter (the gymnast), now the conjoined brothers Harry, Marlon, Arnold, Jackson, Simon, Kent and Susan have vanished without a trace. That be more than half me crew, and the rest be mainly monkeys in dinner jackets that we traded for some men on that island where they eat men that be exchanged for monkeys in dinner jackets. Oddly specific custom.

And every time they vanished it be in the middle of an unnatural mist that did cover the ship, and every one of them did say some strange words to me afore their fate. Things like 'help me, the strange man we picked up is trying to kill me' and 'oh my god, please stop him from biting my neck.' I be making neither head nor tail of them words, strange so they be.

Me only comfort is knowing that England be close and that strange man we picked up be still just as friendly as he ever was.

A Cutting from Whitby Paper 'The Dailygraph', 8th August 1989

STORM BLOWS IN FROM FRENCH WATERS, RUSSIAN SHIP DAMAGES BEACH, BLACK DOG SCARES LOCALS: THE IMMIGRATION CRISIS DEEPENS

A vile French storm has battered the polite little English town of Whitby, tearing slates from roofs and suckling babes from their mothers' arms. The storm was unregistered and unwarranted, yet it came nonetheless and has ruined the town to a state of annoyance. Local officials have declared a state of emergency until tea time while they sort through the rubble from flowerpots blown over. This paper says that this reaction is not enough and demands a full invasion of France.

The storm was accompanied by Russian ship The Demeter sailing carelessly into the harbour and striking the beach with malice, missing some nearby fishermen by a mere half a mile! At the helm was a deceased gentleman who had been lashed to the wheel, no doubt the result of some degenerate Russian parlour game. The only other occupants were a party of well-dressed monkeys having tea and crumpets. Local officials have declared that the ship will be searched thoroughly and the instance of the missing crew and deceased helmsman investigated. This paper says that this reaction is not enough and demands a full invasion of Russia.

Once the ship had become beached a crowd descended to laugh and point at the foreign tragedy. When a policeman prized the hull open through a gash in the side a huge black dog bounded out of the hole and ran away up the beach and became hidden amongst the trees and bushes. Eye-witnesses say the beast was 'huge', 'black' and 'a dog'. Local officials have declared that the beast should be considered dangerous until otherwise confirmed and have asked locals to stay away should they see it. This paper says that this reaction is not enough and demands a full invasion of...erm...wherever it is big black dogs come from. Don't put this in. Why are you still writing? Put the pen down. Stop writing! Stop putting it into an envelope and sealing it! Don't send that to the editor! Don't reopen it to write everything that I've said since you sealed it!

From the Diary of Mina Murray, 10th August 1890

Such strange times we live in, that abandoned Russian ships should become shipwrecked in violent storms while young ladies sleepwalk endlessly and homosexuals stalk the land. Why just the other day I heard tell of these creatures of the night who prey on the youthful and drain their fluids. One has an inkling to write about them in some analogous manner.

The captain of the Demeter has been buried alongside his parrot and favourite peg leg and the search for the big black dog continuous, for though I did not see it myself I am sure from its description that it is a creature of evil. Nothing that was ever big or black was couth.

But my poor sweet Lucy continues to wander about in the night and wakes with such lethargy that she is unable to perform her daily faintings. Yesterday I took her for a long walk up the garden path and showed her my bush, then we wandered into Old Pete's Crack to admire the natural erection beyond the hills, but alas neither the jaunt nor the sights were enough to keep her in her bed that night, not even after spending hours staring at those boobies, for they were nesting in the trees. Young ladies these days.

I shall keep an eye on her tonight for I know, without any good indication, that something terrible may happen to her.

From the Diary of Mina Murray, 11th August 1890

As I write this my breath is short and my heart beats rapidly, for I have witnessed a most terrible sight! Last night I put Lucy to bed and then saw to myself, then I went to bed. But I dreamt of terrible things in the night like votes for women, Australian accents and agnosticism, and so I woke in a start with sweat pouring off my body. Once I had reminded myself that such nightmares do not exist I went to visit Lucy but found her bed empty and the door open and her bedpan full.

I ran out into the night after only a brief moment to put on a sensible dress and coat and adjust my hair in case the vicar should be passing and began my search. After many seconds of looking I spotted her walking vertically up the side of a building and up, over the roof, which I noted as peculiar for a lady at this time of year. I hurried round to the other side and followed her as she made her way to the graveyard outside the church on the hill. There I saw a dark figure waiting for her, one of her suitors I reasoned, for as she approached he bent his head down to her neck and embraced her.

I smiled at the beautiful sight of a woman so in love that she would put her health and life in danger by inducing in herself a hypnotic state that she could sleepwalk through a dark town at night and visit a foreboding man in a graveyard at midnight. But then I noticed that Lucy was groaning and thought it best to back away before things got untidy, but the sound seemed uncomfortable for her and so I stepped forward. The man saw me and I saw him: his eyes, red like blood and fire! His teeth, pointy and sharp like needles! And his brow, clearly evident of a person of malcontent, for physiognomy is true and anyone who says otherwise is a liberal.

In shock and horror I gasped and my mouth fell open, which I then shut again for good manners. The man approached me with malice in his eyes and I shuddered at his approach. Now I am barely able to write with him looming over me, looking puzzled as to why I have not fled or cowered in fear. For the truth is I am so petrified that I can barely write, not to mention I find it uncomfortable to have someone reading over my shoulder. Yes I am talking about you sir. Kindly refrain. Ah, now he has gone, muttering under his breath something like 'women.'

I shall return Lucy to her bed and write to her suitors at once.

From the Diary of Mina Murray, 13th August 1890

Last night I saw a large bat outside Lucy's bedroom window. Not sure why I'm mentioning it.

From the Diary of Mina Murray, 19th August 1890

Jonathon has written to tell me he is setting out for Whitby to be with me once more. I cannot contain my excitement to see his manly moustache. It will take all of my willpower not to wave and smile at him when I see him. Just the thought of such a public display of affection makes me blush.

Meanwhile my dear Lucy continues to walk about at night. I have decided to put a lock on her bedroom door since she met the mysterious gentleman in the graveyard. Once was strange, twice was just silly. When it occurred for the third time I put my foot down and said to myself, 'if this happens just once more I shall have to consider putting a lock on her door!' Well, it only took another two instances of the gentleman biting her neck and drawing blood and sucking it down for me to think long and hard about it.

But alas, though she can no longer wander about the town in twilight she stares out of her window, almost mournfully, and her complexion grows more pallid by the day. I am considering unlocking her door in the daytime to bring her food and water.

From the diary of Dr. Seward, 19th August 1890

Renfield has once again given me cause to write about my concerns, for after today's events I am beginning to wonder about the causes and definitions of 'madness'. Since the incident I shall sensitively refer to as 'the nutjob eats the sparrows' Renfield has shown amazing signs of recovering. Indeed, at one point I entered his room to find him hosting a lecture on advanced calculus to a drawing of a man on the wall he'd made out of faeces.

I had even begun to consider putting him in for tests to evaluate his current state of madness (the 'ooglyboogly-wibble-wibble' exam) when I discovered that he had somehow managed to escape his cell, leaving no clue as to his means of extradition save a note explaining exactly how he did it.

We searched high and low for him, then once we had looked at the ceiling and the floor of his room we decided to go through the enormous hole in the wall and widen the hunt. In retrospect it might have been prudent to fill the hole before we put Renfield into it. After asking around for an escaped madman and getting nothing but joking locals ('you caught me guv, what am I like?' or 'you'll be looking for me husband, har, har, har') we spotted him in the graveyard on the hill, kneeling at a freshly-filled plot and crying out for his 'master'.

We returned him to his room without much difficulty and pulled a rope across the hole with a note politely asking him not to escape again. We then asked around at the half-a-dozen or so masochistic societies that I knew of but no one there was known to Renfield as 'master'. I returned, downhearted and pleasantly bruised, to discuss with my peers the nature of Renfield's state and the meaning behind his sudden deterioration but none of us could come up with any serious notion. One fellow suggested it might be a Transylvanian aristocrat with supernatural powers looking for a thrall to do his bidding, to which the rest of us laughed at his good humour in this grim subject.

I shall keep a closer eye on Renfield from now on and have requested someone check on the rope across the hole no fewer than once a week, lest he make another daring escape.

From the Diary of Mina Murray, 30th August 1890

My dear Lucy has reason to be cheerful in her regrettably melancholic state at last, for she has chosen a suitor and set a date to be married: she has spoken to Arthur Holmwood, son of the very rich Lord Holmwood, and told him that she loves him dearly and would very much like to be very rich, and Arthur has set a date of the 28th September for the marriage. I asked if she would like me to tell the other two gentlemen about her decision for in her delicate state I feared she would succumb further to her symptoms but the brave girl decided she would do it herself. I sat with her as she produced an 'L' shape on her forehead, poked her tongue out and proclaimed 'loser' to Dr. Seward and the American Quincy Morris, who, both being fine gentlemen, waited until they were out of the room before they sobbed like babies and tore their clothes off in despair.

And speaking of marriages, Jonathon, who has been with me now for over a week, has been most persistent that we should be married as soon as possible, so tomorrow will be the happy occasion. Since his trip to Transylvania he has been skittish, reserved and grim, clinging to me like a mollusc. At times he has let his uncouth behaviour be seen in public, holding my hand and glancing at my ankles, and I have had to tell him so but he is persistent in his newfound attachment to me. I have asked him repeatedly what transpired in Transylvania to change him so but he only asks me not to ask him whenever I ask him. I ask myself, is it asking too much to ascribe logic to an askew narrative, a scribble on as crucial a script as this that my husband transcribes to me? Ah, screw it.

From the Correspondence of Dr. Seward to Arthur Holmwood, 1st September 1890

Dear sir, I write to you in the expectation that you are well and have not suffered a grievous wound that would render you unable to marry my ex-suitor Lucy Westenra. For such would be the shame if you were unable to fulfil your duty to her and I had to step up to fill your conniving shoes. Apologies, I meant to write 'convivial' but instead of scribbling it out I decided to leave it in. Just so you know that I am a man who lets the world know what I am capable of.

As requested I have attended to dear Lucy and examined her but I'll be violently intercoursed if I know what's wrong with her. She exhibits signs of melancholy, a viable medical condition in this day and age that will probably never be looked back upon with ridicule. She looks about sadly when awake and comments on things in a lamentable way, which is awfully depressing. I have prescribed cocaine to brighten her moods and heroin, because why not? It's not like it does any long-term damage.

But before I leave to smoke copious amounts of opium, a pastime I thoroughly encourage as a doctor to all and sundry, I must inform you that I have notified Lucy's odd condition to my colleague Dr. Van Helsing of Holland, who is an expert in pale-skinned young ladies, unless there's a jury present in which case he most certainly isn't and never has been. The doctor tells me he shall be arriving shortly and looks forward to examining Lucy thoroughly.

From the Correspondence of Dr. Seward to Van Helsing, Amsterdam, 4th September, 1890

Dear friend and colleague, it is with a happy heart that I write to inform you that Lucy Westenra, the young lady who's figure I have described for you in charcoal and dried pasta glued to parchment, has made an almost miraculous recovery. Why, just yesterday she was walking about without a reflection and yet today she is on fine form, laughing and joking and pushing beggars over in the street. I daresay your services will no longer be needed, thank heavens, though I appreciate you undertaking the journey to come.

Wherever this letter finds you I hope it will not be of too much trouble for you to make your way back home.

Sincerely, Dr. Seward (copyright Stoker, Bram)

From the Correspondence of Van Helsing MD, DPH, D. Lit, etc. etc. to Seward, 4th September 1890

Dearest and respected colleague, though indeed my journey hath already begun I am pleased to cancel it on such joyous news. I have had to leave my taxi on a dirt road and traipse back to Amsterdam on foot, becoming drenched and covered in mud in a sudden downpour on the way, but what is a little discomfort on my part when your friend Lucy is relieved of her own?

Sincerely, Van Helsing

From the Correspondence of Dr. Seward to Van Helsing, Amsterdam, 5th September, 1890

Alas dear friend, I apologise for this reply to your reply but I am afraid that Lucy's condition has deteriorated since my last letter. As I write I can see her thin pallor has returned and she no longer tries to swat my hand away as I try to grope her. Something is terribly wrong and I must ask for your assistance, once again. My dearest thanks in advanced old friend.

Sincerely, Dr. Seward

From the Correspondence of Van Helsing MD, DPH, D. Lit, etc. etc. to Seward, 5th September 1890

Such an unfortunate turn of events, both for myself and also Lucy, that she must swing between conditions so and I must resume my journey. I had only just poured myself a cup of tea after getting out of my wet clothes before your letter arrived. But I suppose it is of the utmost importance that I arrive as soon as I am able, so I have packed the remainder of my clothes and am setting off once more. I shall see thee soon old friend.

Sincerely, Van Helsing

From the Correspondence of Dr. Seward to Van Helsing, Amsterdam, 6th September, 1890

What luck! Though I daresay less so for you old friend, for you see Lucy has brightened up again almost as quickly as she darkened. No need for you to journey again. I hope your reversal is not so bad as previous.

Sincerely, Dr. Seward

From the Correspondence of Van Helsing MD, DPH, D. Lit, etc. etc. to Seward, 6th September 1890

I am beginning to wonder who is having the worse luck? The afflicted girl or the yo-yoing old man. No matter, Lucy's health is what is most important I should say, and though the ferry captain would not turn the vessel around for me I was able to swim to a nearby ferry going back to Holland. I hesitate to say it but...please keep me informed of Lucy's condition.

Sincerely, Van Helsing

From the Correspondence of Dr. Seward to Van Helsing, Amsterdam, 7th September, 1890

The funniest thing has happened dear friend. You'll laugh when I tell you: little Lucy is heavy and grim again, drained of the joys of life. Therefore could you possibly be a dear and turn yourself around? There's a good chap. What a jolly runabout we've put you on!

Sincerely, Dr. Seward

From the Correspondence of Van Helsing MD, DPH, D. Lit, etc. etc. to Seward, 7th September 1890

Having no dry clothes and no available ferry to make the return journey I have been very, very tempted to turn my heel and go home. But I am a doctor and I took an oath that makes no sense so I have managed to barter my way aboard a vessel carrying excrement to England, so that I might see to Lucy. If your next letter is anything other than house rules for my visit I shall be inclined to lose my temper, such that it is.

Sincerely, Van Helsing

From the Correspondence of Dr. Seward to Van Helsing, Amsterdam, 8th September, 1890

Now then, the thing is dear friend...

From the Correspondence of Van Helsing MD, DPH, D. Lit, etc. etc. to Seward, 8th September 1890

Stop! I won't hear any more.

From the Correspondence of Dr. Seward to Van Helsing, Amsterdam, 8th September, 1890

But Lucy is well again and...

From the Correspondence of Van Helsing MD, DPH, D. Lit, etc. etc. to Seward, 8th September 1890

Stop writing this instant!

From the Correspondence of Dr. Seward to Van Helsing, Amsterdam, 8th September, 1890

But...

From the Correspondence of Van Helsing MD, DPH, D. Lit, etc. etc. to Seward, 8th September 1890

Shush! If I have to infect Lucy with a flesh-eating virus myself just to justify my journey then God help me I will do it! I have been soaked twice, caked in mud once and caked in a completely different and far fouler brown substance since, not to mention the number of times I fell over while yawning into one of the many piles of the brown material, so do not say another word to me or I will be forced to rip your head off and use it as a latrine.

Looking forward to seeing you soon.

Cordially, Van Helsing

From the Diary of Mina Harker, 9th September 1890

I have met the strange, eccentric and quite possibly psychopathic Dr. Van Helsing and I feel assured that Lucy is now in safe, sensible hands. When the doctor arrived the first thing he did was remove all his clothes. He told us it was because he was wet but I am more inclined to believe it is some ancient shamanistic Dutch tradition. Once he had covered up his mentionables we visited Lucy in her bedroom so that the doctor could examine her.

I never realised just how supple Lucy was but the doctor was keen to point it out often and under his breath. The next thing he did was to announce that Lucy's blood was bad and that she needed a transfusion from a live host. Of course we all volunteered immediately, seeing no problem with allowing ourselves to share blood with a victim of an obviously dangerous virus. But it was Lucy's fiancé Arthur Holmwood who's offer was accepted, for he is to be married to her after all and they should probably get used to sharing bodily fluids.

Arthur is to sit in her room tonight, attached to her from vein to vein via a 'tube' (my poor woman's mind cannot comprehend such advanced terminology) but we are also to hang garlic around her room. The doctor insists it is to ward off certain elements that may do her harm from without but I have a sneaking suspicion it's to hide the fact that he smells of shit.

From the Diary of Mina Harker, 10th September 1890

Oh what a tragedy! Lucy's mother took the garlic down in the night and now all we can smell is Van Helsing, who so far has refused to bathe.

Oh yes, and also the transfusion worked and Lucy is brighter than she has been these past few weeks but she also had a weird dream where a wolf broke in and killed her mother and as it turns out her mother is actually dead. What an odd coincidence. Amusing really, in a morbid way.

Doctors Seward and Helsing examined the body of Lucy's mother and confirmed that she was dead by taking her pulse and examining her pupils and prodding her body with a stick. Lucy is distraught, naturally, because she hates the smell of poo but also she really loved her mother. I have tried to comfort her by offering to have her mother stuffed and mounted over the fireplace but Lucy was ill-mannered in her response and I was unable to understand what she was saying through snot and tears and unladylike bawling. I shall reprimand her later for her behaviour in front of the men, who remained stoic throughout, only fidgeting to readjust the pegs on their noses.

Meanwhile I believe Dr. Seward would like to write something in his own diary.

From the Diary of Dr. Seward, 15th September 1890

My thanks to you Mrs. Harker, for though our entries are 5 days apart I am sure that no one else will have written anything during that time that will come between us if our diaries were ever to be collated to uncover a sinister truth that we are all party to without realising it.

And with that I move onto grim subjects, for indeed Lucy's condition has stabilised but only with the continued influx of fresh blood. Poor Arthur has given all he can and so I offered myself as the next chattel and was due to link myself to Lucy tonight, but something has come up which I cannot ignore:

You remember Renfield? I mentioned him several excerpts back, he's the crazy man who ate the sparrows. Anyway, while sitting in my office this afternoon with my feet up pretending to work I heard a shuffling at the door. Of course I immediately made myself look busy but before I could invite the outsider in the door was flung open and there stood Renfield in the altogether holding a sharp knife in one hand. He had a mad look in his eyes that suggested he was not all there at that moment, that and the fact that he had smeared faeces all over himself.

I asked him politely what he was doing, for it wasn't Wednesday when he usually covers himself in faecal matter, but without another word he lunged at me, swinging wildly and trying to stab me. Thankfully he was trying to stab me with the hand that didn't contain the knife, but once he realised this he brought the knife across me with a slash and struck my wrist.

Blood jettisoned immediately from my wound and it was all I could do to not think of a romantic poem to write before I died. I had to survive, for Lucy, she needed this blood, so I clamped my mouth around it and began to suck. At this sight Renfield stopped and stared, eventually saying 'you're disgusting' as he rubbed poo into his armpits.

The orderlies came and took him away after a while, leaving me to write this entry in my diary, which isn't easy considering the paper keeps getting drenched in blood. If this keeps up I'll never get around to sealing off this wound!

From the Diary of Van Helsing, 18th September 1890

Such dire times we live in, that little Lucy should degrade with each passing day though we give her the best blood and most charming recitals of Shakespeare's bloodiest tragedies. Honestly, you'd think she'd crack a smile when Caesar is stabbed to death but no, nothing. She persists in her melancholic illness and, though I have yet to express my fears openly, I believe she may die within a day or so.

I realise now my mistake at having written this as I always read aloud what I am writing as I write it, and now everyone in the room knows that Lucy is on her last legs. A bit nosey, if you ask me. Especially that Jonathon Harker, what a nosey busybody he is.

I realise now my mistake for the second time, as the good and brave and lovely Jonathon Harker has grabbed me by the throat and is glaring down his bushy moustache at me. I, of course, meant what I said before as a jest and...urgh...choke! Choke! Gag!

My habit of reading what I write works in reverse too.

From the Diary of the American Quincy Morris, 18th September 1890

Dear diary, just thought I'd write something down as everyone else seems to be doing it.

From the Diary of Dr. Seward, 20th September 1890

The day has come. Poor Lucy has passed away. We maintained the transfusions, administered daily by myself, Van Helsing, Jonathon Harker, the American Quincy Morris and Lucy's betrothed Arthur Holmwood, but to no avail. She was too weak it seems and she faded completely mere moments after receiving one last kiss from her beloved Arthur.

Naturally we all agreed that this was a suspicious coincidence so we had Arthur arrested for murder.

In the mean time Van Helsing has been pestering me about cutting off Lucy's head and driving a wooden stake through her heart, which I obviously scoffed at for, as we all know, such a privilege is reserved for the husband alone and he is currently under arrest for cold-blooded murder, the monster. No, any head cutting shall have to wait until we've had our lunch.

From the Diary of Mina Harker, 22nd September 1890

Unable to stand the misery of Whitby any longer I departed with Jonathon for London no sooner had Lucy's body been interred and her worldly possessions fought over in a cage match. I, with my new dress and broken nose, was happy to know that she was finally at rest and could no longer be troubled by this world and it's liberal demons. I naturally assume this because there was seemingly nothing supernatural about her illness or death.

The journey was uneventful so I slept for the entirety of it, and therefore am unable to verify that the distance between London and Whitby and the length of time between Lucy's passing and now is sufficient to allow for that journey to have been made and I, the writer, do not feel sufficient inclination to check and research it. If you are reading this and consider it a cop out, you can spin on this.

However, while out walking today with Jonathon on the busy streets of London my dearest husband took a queer turn. It was very camp, he had his arm out and upturned and his hips swayed greatly from side to side. But once he had turned into the next street he stopped suddenly as though frozen by something which would make a man do so. I asked him what was wrong but he didn't reply, only pointing and replying "There he is, the man himself." I followed his finger but it was aimed at the floor next to his foot. It was only then I noticed, further down the street and obscured from my vision by Jonathon's other hand that was clenched with only his index finger out, a strange man with pale skin and jet-black hair. He had a wicked look about him and he was tall and slender, as all wicked men are, and I knew immediately that Jonathon was terrified of him because whenever he was terrified he smelled of urine.

Later, once I had calmed him down and he had changed out of his terrified trousers, I asked him to elaborate on the man he had seen but he only shook his head and told me that such things should never be known. Seeing no reason to doubt my husband I put the entire event behind me and have even now forgotten what it entailed. What was I even saying? What have I been writing about? Who am I writing to? Why do I keep detailing impossible events without questioning them thoroughly?

From the Diary of Jonathon Harker, 23rd September 1890

It has been such a long time since I wrote in my diary but I feel that now is the most appropriate moment to reveal what happened to me in Transylvania seeing as Lucy has succumbed to her seemingly supernatural illness, though I am sure my own supernatural experiences in similar circumstances would have had no impact on her recovery with the supernatural expert Van Helsing on hand.

My dearest Mina, I write this to you in the expectation that no one else will read this. To that extent I include this crude drawing of my genitals. It is accurate, as you will attest. I would also like to thank you for loving me despite my tendency for wearing little girls dresses about the house. Knowing that no one apart from you will read this, especially not thousands around the globe in the form of a bestselling novel, makes me content to include such personal secrets here.

But alas, though I have been happy spinning around in my little pink dress you will know Mina that my mind has been haunted by my experiences in Transylvania and up until now I have not dared to reveal the awful truths to you, for fear that in so doing they will drive you mad with anguish. That's a thing that can happen.

But after seeing 'him' yesterday I can go on no longer without someone else knowing the extent of my misery. Mina, once you have read this I implore you to go back and read the rest but make sure you skip over any bits where other ladies are concerned. There's nothing wrong in those sections it's just that they deal with blood and gore and other things that you wouldn't enjoy. No need to read into them in detail, my dearest, most beloved, cherished of my heart.

And once you are done come back to me. I shall be sitting in front of the fireplace with a grim, veil-piercing stare.

From the Correspondence of Mina Harker to Van Helsing, 24th September 1890

Esteemed friend Van Helsing, I write to you with grave information: 24D, that's where Lucy's body is buried. But I also come to you with Dire news: Mr. Dire has opened a new shop in Liverpool Street. It is quite charming. Alas, not all my news is good though, for I also have to tell you a dark secret, which is that if you close your eyes before stepping into the dark it will help you see better because your pupils will already be expanded.

Oh yes, and Jonathon met a shape-shifting man in Transylvania that he didn't think was of any interest to anyone. He has consistently refused to tell me anything of his travels until yesterday, when he passed me his diary without a word and left me to read it. What I found was shocking and quite a strain on my womanly mind. He used such words as 'blood', 'castle' and 'and', concepts that my feminine sensibilities have much trouble handling. His handwriting was also very masculine and I had to stop several times as I was getting hot flushes.

The point is though, and I'm paraphrasing greatly because it's actually all a bit long-winded and could probably have been summarised much better, Jonathon was the guest of a man who was, at the time, old and frail yet just the other day Jonathon spotted that same man in London looking as though he were at the height of his youth.

I know that you are an expert in the illogical and make-believe so I thought I'd come to you for advice and to also point out the obvious similarities between my husband's experience and those of Lucy, for I fear that these very obvious similarities that were obviously apparent are somehow connected. What do you think?

Hugs and kisses,

Mina Harker

From the Correspondence of Van Helsing to Mina Harker, 26th September 1890

My dear lady, I have read your letter and am convinced of a theory I had but which until now was absolutely outrageous: thankfully upon hearing that your husband saw someone he recognised in London it has proven everything correct. Now who's the lunatic Professor Bumblebee? I must insist that both you and Jonathon come to Whitby immediately because we can't play a good game of Twister with only 4 people, plus it would make the game far more interesting if we had a female joining in. For science, you understand.

While you are here you might as well join us on a midnight errand involving Lucy's grave. Do not be alarmed my dear, for I know that upon seeing the word 'grave' you are wont to feint in horror, and probably once again on seeing that word too. Once you have roused yourself I beseech you: do not be afraid, for our business with Lucy will be completely sanitary, though not particularly sane.

Big smiley face,

Van Helsing

From the Diary of Dr. Seward, 29th September 1890

Oh Lord in Heaven above, I call upon you to take away my eyes, that I may never look upon this cursed Earth again since the sights I have witnessed seem capable of driving me to madness. I ask thee, also, to help me to not be so overdramatic and theatrical when writing in my own personal diary. Many thanks.

But now to the retelling, and such a retelling! It all began on the 3rd of May 1890, when Jonathon Harker began his journal on his visit to Transylvania. I would write it all out again or provide a summary but if it so please you, whomsoever is reading this, then you can break into Mr. Harker's house and find the script itself. You have my express permission. He keeps the key under the pot plant.

Suffice to say that once Jonathon and Mina had recounted the entire terrible narrative to us we were amazed and horrified, but mostly we thought 'wouldn't this make for a ripping yarn? I bet it would make a lot of money in 100 years time when it's being fleeced for every penny.' Van Helsing seemed to take express interest in the descriptions of the Count, however, and stopped Jonathon on several occasions to ask questions such as 'did he have pointed teeth?', 'did he shy away from sunlight?' and 'what colour were his underpants?' (The answer to all three was 'Mexican cheese' bizarrely) When the tale was over Van Helsing took to pacing the room with his finger on his chin and his other hand scratching his nether regions. Seeing him in such a considered state of thought we did nothing to disturb him, save for the fireworks and drum-solo competition. But eventually he turned to us all with a finger raised in the air.

"My friendsh," he said in his hilarious Dutch accent. "Thish ish a terrible shituashion we find ourshelvesh in, for the tashk ahead fill be neizer eashy nor happy." He then went on to explain that we faced an adversary who was beyond logic and sanity, a man who preyed upon the young under cover of darkness. At that all us men reached for our weapons and brought them to Van Helsing's neck, but then he furthered that by saying it was someone 'other' than he who coincidentally fitted that description. Our weapons sheathed, Van Helsing's head drooped as he paused and let the firelight dance across his face in a dramatic manner. It was even more effective as he played his violin for emphasis.

It was then that the greatest shock hit us: Van Helsing sneezed and didn't cover his mouth! We were all aghast! After the several hours it took to recover our senses and bring Mina back to sanity Van Helsing gathered us again and apologised before informing us of the task ahead: to combat the demonic villain before us we had to perform a most diabolical act on the body of one we loved. At this Jonathon stood up and proudly announced that he was willing to do anything to dispose of our foe as he dropped his pantaloons and prepared himself for his wife, but then Van Helsing calmly told him he was mistaken and asked the American Quincy Morris to stop sketching.

No, the dreaded act we were to perform involved sweet Lucy, her breast and a long wooden object. None of us knew exactly what he had in mind but we all had a pretty good idea.

And so we ventured to the graveyard where Lucy was buried, in the family tomb of the Holmwood's alongside Arthur's departed father, mother and a local Chinese man called 'Larry'. There we watched and waited as the usual occupants of a graveyard went about their nightly routine, drunks, zombies and ghosts, nothing out of the ordinary. Until Van Helsing pointed out a familiar figure wandering between the headstones looking for all the world like our own dear Lucy, except there must have been some mistake! For I witnessed her being interred myself and checked her pulse whence she was dead (probably should have checked it once or twice while she was alive. Live and learn) And yet there she was. We watched silently, daring not to blow our party horns even once, as she glided towards her tomb and there slipped like a piece of paper through the tiny crack at the edge of the door. We wondered two things: how this was possible and why she didn't use the door itself as we had left it open after examining the tomb earlier.

We then approached the tomb and entered, none of us daring to breath. Of course we lost consciousness because you need oxygen to stay alive, but once we had recovered we looked inside. To our surprise, where earlier Lucy's body lay on the slab where we had left her, now she was there on the slab where we had left her! I suppose it might be pertinent to point out that we had been in since then and noticed the body not being there. That is probably important to the revelation.

Regardless, there she was, as pale as ever she had been in the last weeks of her life and yet more alive. She had a nasty sneer on her face which confirmed Van Helsing's suspicions immediately: she was a vampire, a bloodsucking undead creature. Facial features never lie. To that end Van Helsing produced a steak and we all gasped as he brought it close to Lucy's body, then ate it. Apparently he was very hungry. Once he had finished he then withdrew a wooden peg from his bag o' stuff and a hammer and told us what was to happen next: one of us would place the point of the peg upon Lucy's breast, over her heart, and hammer it until it entered her body. Of course we all giggled at the imagery but then we composed ourselves as we had to decide who would do the grim act. We drew straws but Arthur Holmwood won (lucky bastard) and so, with a single tear in his eye, he said goodbye to Lucy once more and drove the wooden peg into her heart.

What a shock we had when Lucy came to life, gasped out in pain and cried "ow! You stabbed me through the heart!" But just as soon as it had begun the event ceased, and Lucy's body stiffened like a stiff thing. Stranger still, once the act was complete Lucy's face finally seemed to look at peace and rested and we knew we had done the right thing. Arthur, naturally, was greatly disturbed by the incident and so we left him in the tomb to reconcile himself. The poor man was clearly very upset but we endeavoured to let him get it all out of his system as he screamed from behind the locked tomb door.

And now we are back in this place, wherever it is exactly that we have been meeting in Whitby these past few months, almost as if Lucy's pegging had never happened. Yet it had, difficult as it was to believe, but Van Helsing tells us this is only the beginning. There is a greater evil beyond Whitby, itself a most heinous place even before the undead stalked its streets, that resides in London, if Jonathon's unbelievable story is to be believed. Our next recourse, Van Helsing continued, is to gather together the incessant writing we have all been doing and combine it into a cohesive and rambling narrative of events that, while seemingly unrelated at the time, were miraculously recorded in impossibly accurate detail despite the diminishing returns of recall and yet contains no information that wouldn't be pertinent to the matter at hand.

We have, of course, elected Mrs. Harker to the task of transcribing all our work into a single thread and to help her along we all gave her an encouragingly patronising pat on the rear. I don't know how Mrs. Murray felt about the arrangement because she was hidden behind mountains of paper.

From the Diary of Mina Harker, 30th September 1890

Having sifted through the endless reams of paper the men have given me I have finally managed to combine them into a single thread. I did offer to summarise the facts to make it easier to read owing to the dangerous nature of our task and the need for concise action, but they insisted that it remain rambling with dramatic tension and character arcs. And now comes the reading, for each of us must now commit to memory every single word of what has been written but we are all confident we can do it because the task ahead is so great, therefore we know that our fallible human minds will somehow muster up super-human abilities that cannot be explained by science but which will seem awfully romantic in years to come.

After the reading was done it was Van Helsing's turn again to talk to us about impossible creatures of nightmares. Of course we found it all hard to believe, that there could be shape-shifting men in this world created by a giant glowing man in the sky who is also a different man and a dove. But believe it we must, for we have already seen impossible things in these dark few months like rude Dutchmen and that sparrow with the bowler hat and monocle that I saw the other day who ignored me when I said 'good day' to it.

Van Helsing spoke of vampires or vampyres, depending on how edgy you wish your lore to be, humans who were once alive but now are dead though they stalk the Earth yet in search of innocent living humans to claim. They were creatures of impossible feats, able to change their bodies into bats, dogs and malleable mist though Van Helsing is sure he once spied a vampire he was hunting disguised as a woman's intimate device. To what end he could not tell, though I think we all had a pretty good idea.

They also possess powers of supernatural persuasion, able to convince others of untruths like 'the monarchy is a falsehood' and 'one day a woman with a large posterior will be worth her weight in gold, of which at least 80% will be said posterior.'

With mouths agape and legs akimbo we all began to slowly comprehend the creeping horror that had slowly engulfed us all without any obvious warnings. Our foe was one such as this, a creature from beyond both the veil and mortal ken, who's shrewdness in scheming was matched only by his decadent bloomers.

"What must we do heer Helsing? If this creature of evil possesses such powers how can we mere mortal men (and a lady no less!) hope to end his torrent of terror?"

"To thish I haff two reshponshesh. Firshtly, nishe alliteration to add dramatic tension. Shecondly, do not deshpair! For I haff a shcheme of my own to outdo this dark… sorry, *thish* dark creature but it will require all off our witsh."

And so we huddled together to hear the mad doctor's mad plan and, later, play a couple of quick games of Bridge.

From the Diary of Mina Harker, 2nd October 1890

I write today in anticipation of my role within Van Helsing's grand reprisal of the count, which is to say I am being put into a corner where I can do no harm to myself, silly girl. My womanly being, being a bing on his radar, a bee in his bonnet, because I alone can offer him what he has lost and thus craves with ever greater hunger, namely the body of a woman. He has tried, as the doctor assures us, to wear panties and stockings himself but his slender vampiric figure does not pass itself off well as a buxom woman of the West and so his attention, originally drawn to poor sweet bountifully-boobied Lucy, will inevitably be diverted to me, the next logical lady in the chain of ladyness.

After a short but very detailed hands-on lecture about why the count would lust for my breasts we decided that I should be removed from the equation, though after some gentle haggling Jonathon worked the men down from metal pipes to a simple sedative that doctor Seward would administer.

So while the men prepare for a daring adventure into the very heart of evil itself (the main street of Carfax) I have set out my toilet and made my bed so that I might slumber peacefully in chemically-induced rest. Isn't God marvellous for inventing science for us to discover?

I hand over now to the men, I presume, who's next passage will be undoubtedly more exciting than my own, though I did engage in a most impressive wrestling match with my blouse just now.

From the Diary of Dr. Seward, 4th October 1890

I find, for the first time in such a while, a moment of respite in which to record the happenings of the recent past. In between vampires, blasphemous lunatics and the occasional jig I have completely neglected my diary, an oversight I shall remedy, presently, indubitably.

So it was that, with Mina safely defenceless in a house by herself with no way to detect intruders, we gentlemen set out to thwart the devil from Transylvania and send him back to the hell from whence he came: Europe. Having gathered information about his antics we deduced that he was storing coffins full of defiled earth in an abandoned abbey off the main street, so there we attended with weapons in tow and as much tea as we could stomach to brew at this ungodly hour.

The abbey was deathly quiet, almost as though something evil had been happening there, which it had, so it made sense in retrospect, which made that entire train of thought utterly pointless. We found in the basement of the abbey a coffin, wrought in evil wood and shut with evil nails. We eschewed the complementary evil biscuits the count had left out for visitors and set to work.

Prizing open the first coffin we found it empty, not a thing inside, save for a few tonnes of earth compacted within. We all knew what to do next, and after we had all had some jolly fun teabagging the count's bed Van Helsing produced from his pocket a holy wafer. Well, he pulled something else out first but that was much less sacred.

He placed the wafer slowly onto the earth and muttered a prayer under his breath (in Latin of course, we're not poor people going to poor heaven!) and with that, he said, the deed was done. As simple as that: placing some bread-transmogrified-into-the-literal-body-of-God-made-mortal onto a load of mud. We sighed with relief, then turned round to see the rest of the coffins and that sigh turned into a very English grumble. Well, the Englishmen grumbled. The American Quincy Morris fired his pistols into the air and danced in frustration.

But soon enough we had made all of the count's defiled coffins re-filed. A job well done, we prepared to ascend and get blackout drunk at the local whore house when a shadow blocked our way. I recognised it at once, first by the stench, second by the distinct dangling bit between its legs.

"Renfield," I called out, for it was he. "What are you doing out at this time of night? Isn't it about time you ought to be thrashing about in bed and screaming about your night terrors?"

But all was silent, save for the flies buzzing about his excrement-laden body. I tensed up and leant to one side, whispering a plan of action in Jonathon's ear but I haphazardly licked it a few dozen times and he failed to get the gist of what

I was saying. But just then Renfield spoke, and it was in such a voice that I had never heard before, as cold and sane as ever a man had spoken.

"My master is here, he is come."

"Who is your master, Renfield? May we have three guesses?"

"What is the prize?" piped up Jonathon.

Suddenly there was a 'whoosh' and a 'whirl' and a 'wham-bam-ba-loo-ba-a-wham-bam-boo' and darkness descended upon us. We were thrown into a black cloud of fear and methane (apologies gentlemen) as insurmountable dread consumed us, but from within the void I heard a voice cry out valiantly, "Begone devil! Heed my wordsh!" And then the sound of hissing as the darkness slowly faded away, leaving us men where we had stood. There was Van Helsing, holding aloft a crucifix as like a shield, the source of the count's banishment. He also had a Jewish menorah, a copy of the Quran and some Buddhist prayer beads. "Jusht in cashe," he said.

At the top of the stairs we found the crumpled ruin of the man once known as Renfield, but whom we shall now refer to as 'that naked faecal-covered weirdo' out of reverence for the dead. His cadaver was covered in claw marks and the bones were broken in every conceivable place, I might even venture to suggest that the count shoved extra bones into the poor man just so he could break more of them.

And so after a respectable burial of appropriate length and having spent the rest of that minute making hilarious shadow puppets with our hands and genitalia, returned to Mina and the inevitable safety she would undoubtedly be in.

But alas, woe to our folly, for it was not so upon our return. All was at first well and Mina was soundly asleep, as deep in her slumber as to not notice the hands of Van Helsing checking her body thoroughly. Thrice, in fact. But then, a gasp from the doctor! There upon her neck were two pricks of blood, the icky red stuff still wet and shiny.

"Fiddlesticks!" said I.

"Blast!" said Jonathon.

"Oh for fucks sake!" said the American Quincy Morris.

We all agreed that this indeed was a woman in need, a further kerfuffle to add to the long list of tribulations we had experienced since Jonathon left this Great Britain, which itself must surely be a lesson for all Monarchy-fearing patriots: everything outside this green land is terrible. No exceptions. Croissants, turbans and fireworks, all of it should be rounded up and shot, so says I.

We roused Mina from her peace with a rousing chorus of God Save the Current-Presiding-Monarch and she, bleary-eyed, rose to tell us of the nightmare she had dreamt. In her sleep she saw a grim scene wherein her body, piloted by unknown forces, crept along a dark alleyway. She deftly skipped over a puddle of urine, the stench of it shocking her greatly for it was as though the very water itself were in her nostrils, a fate she had hoped never to have to relive, not since the third time.

As such she had wandered and came to realise she was stalking the dark streets of Carfax, their sights and sounds eerily precise down to the last peeping tom. Suddenly she came upon the very place she knew we were to be investigating that night, the abandoned abbey off the main street. As she entered she heard voices and recognised them as our own, ranking them in order of how much they repulsed her (the results may shock you!), but far from relief she began to feel a powerful sense of anger, growing into fear and then surprise, followed by shock, timidness, intrigue, passion, elucidation, feverement, obstination, disinterest, amazement, obsequiousness, surprise again, and then finally, malice. It was an emotion that devoured her heart and consumed her soul, and she knew then that she was touching the heart of the Devil himself: she was inside the count!

Excuse me, I just allowed myself a moment to titter. A childish notion crept into my head at that wording, but I have just cleared my throat so now you know I mean to go in my previous serious tone.

Yes! She was seeing what he saw and feeling what he felt, both physical and mentical, and she knew then that the rage burning inside her was a result of hearing the voices of those whom he knew were seeking to thwart his machinations, namely 'us' (Jonathon Harker, Arthur Holmwood, the American Quincy Morris and myself, Dr. Seward, in case anybody reading this has found the characters blend into each other and had forgotten them all).

And so Mina unwillingly descended into the darkness of the abbey to finally put an end to the men who were making themselves a nuisance of the count, but found her way blocked by none other than Renfield. She recognised him at once, for obvious reasons which have been hammered to death by now. 'Yes, he was naked and covered in faeces, we get it!' I hear you cry. But on hearing the poor deluded man reveal the approach of the count a new anger flared up in him, namely betrayal. With a hiss and a swish of his cloak in a gay manner the count brought about the place a darkness and yet his eyes could still see as plainly as though it were day. He bounded forward and brought his terrible strength to bare on the poor Renfield, breaking his body in every conceivable way. Why, he even grabbed his nose between two fingers then slapped those two fingers down rather sharpish, causing the fellow all sorts of mischief. And through it all Mina was forced to observe the horror with nary a single kernel of popped corn to enjoy.

And when the man had ceased to be Mina's eyes turned to the men gathered hence, but after taking a single step forwards Van Helsing, the bastard (Mina herself put great emphasis on this word), produced an assortment of religious iconography and the count, disgusted by the hypocrisy, departed taking his black gas with him. And the obscuring mist.

She watched still as the count took to the air, soaring over the rooftops of Carfax and up towards the moon it seemed, by what means she could not tell for she was engaged with the safety demonstration the count was reading from a pamphlet. And then she woke, brought back to her senses by the grim hands of fate to witness four grown men butcher the national anthem. We were intrigued by who these strange men could be, who had seemingly been in the room while we were all singing angelically. But it is not so important for now. The fact is Mrs. Murray has seen through the eyes of the devil himself, and subsequent sleepy-night-night occasions have taught us that this is a regular occurrence. For whenever slumber takes her she thereafter wakes to tell us of his movements, funky as they be.

Until last night, when she tells us the count is ensconced in blackness. But it is not the abyss, alas that his end should not have come so soon, for she can feel a swaying motion as that of being on a ship, and she can hear waves lapping against wood as that of hitting the side of a ship, and she can smell salt water as that which might float a ship. We sat for hours by candlelight trying to figure it out until at last, with first light streaming through the curtains, Arthur jumped up and exclaimed "The count is aboard a ship!" Huzzah! We all gave him a pat on the back and a round of shots was ordered, then while Mina cleared the bullet casings away we men proceeded to plot the count's probable movements.

I see that Dr. Van Helsing is eager to write, for as we have established no two people can be writing at the same time otherwise it makes the apparent narrative very confusing indeed, and so far we've ensured that it is certainly not a rambling mess.

So I shall cease writing forthwith. I see his pen is hoisted above paper, ready to jot. Well I shall stop writing… right about… nnnnnnnnnnnnnnnnnnnnnnnnnnnnnnnnnnnnnnnnnnnnnnnnnnnnnnnn nnnnnnnnnnnnnnnnnnnnnnnnnnnnnnnnnnnnnnnnnnnnnnnnnnnnnnnn nnnnnnnnnnnnnnnnnnnnnnnnnnnnnnnnnnnnnnnnnnnnnnnnnnnnnnnn nnnnnnnnnnow.

From the Diary of Van Helsing, 4th October 1890

My thanks Dr. Seward, which I write in anticipation of you reading this when all good deeds are done. I must say I'm looking forward to going back over this ripping yarn, I can't wait to see what wonderful things you've all been writing about me.

But now to the matter at hand, that of the count. After we discovered that the count was indeed seabound we set about coordinating his journey that we might intersect it ourselves, for though he has left British shores his evil, if left unchecked, shall spread throughout Europe and claim millions of innocents. My compatriots did not seem too bothered by this, but a mere mention of 'invasion' and they were on their feet espousing his villainous ways.

He has no doubt decided to return to Transylvania where he can lick his wounds and touch up his tender parts, but upon his return he will be untouchable (in the metaphorical sense, he was always untouchable in polite society). We must therefore endeavour to cut him off and meet the villain while he is exposed.

Eww!

Arthur, in his capacity as 'rich', has spread out his feelers and come up with a few favours that are owed him for…acts he performed in the past. He remained strangely quiet when quizzed on this but the list of names was sizeable.

Making a mental note to investigate more thoroughly in private at the sauna, I carried on with the foundations of our plan. For I told them the dark man's greatest enemy was not the stake, nor the prospect of votes for women, but the Sun himself, his rays being deadly to the count. Jonathon pointed out that he had seen the count in broad daylight in London but I ignored this as it did not fit with everything else we had established and, also, I couldn't be bothered to think of a reason why it should be. But nevertheless, the Sun is our main weapon against him. The briefest of moments exposed to its full glare will end his endless days for good.

So spoke I, Van Helsing, whom I am told sounds much cooler than it turns out I actually am.

From the Diary of Mina Harker, 11th October 1890

Our sea-based pursuit of the devil is arduous indeed and we are now down to our last few teabags. At this rate we shall have to turn back for more supplies!

In similar frustration my nightly visions have proven fruitless, witnessing only blackness for nigh on two weeks so that our foe remains, though undoubtedly at sea, un-locatable. For all we know he could be bobbing up and down in a bath in Twickenham! Hmm…I shall put this to the men.

From the Diary of Mina Harker, 11th October 1890

While the idea of attending a bath roused their hearts we all agreed that it was a silly notion and that I were a silly girl and should get back to my silly duty of sleeping. I noted to slap myself on the wrist for being so silly, but my womanly strength being what it is could only manage a light brush. Paradoxically my womanly strength meant that the assault floored me and I was rushed to the sick bed by Dr. Seward who dutifully administered the kiss of life, 'just to be sure' he repeated several times.

I shall take this opportunity to slumber awhile and hope that our diabolical friend, or 'fiend' if you will allow me the hilarious pun, has made land somewhere.

From the Diary of Mina Harker, 12th October 1890

My goodness! The count has left the seas and is once again travelling by…err…coffin. But the point is that he is ashore once more, for sure! I dreamt last night the familiar blackness but where previously the sounds and smells of the sea filled my other senses now it was the grinding of wooden wheels on dirt. I could hear all around the nattering of folk in a language I could not understand, but though I had never heard it before and had no idea who was talking it sounded frightfully evil to me, for they used the letter K quite often and rolled their R's.

My guess is that these might be the same locals that haunted the lands around Dracula's haunted castle so I shall endeavour to describe the dialect to Jonathon. But I must do so quickly, for time is of the essence. Every second I spend writing this down instead of taking action our enemy moves further away, so I should probably stop writing and get to it.

Yes, that is a capital idea. Well done me. Whoops! Not too much vanity now or I'll be damned to Hell for all eternity to pay dearly for my minor crimes.

From the Diary of Arthur Holmwood, 5th November 1890

Soon, very soon all our efforts will have come to a brutal and final end, and evil once more vanquished from this world. But enough about the inevitable decline of women's suffrage, Dracula is close by and more vulnerable than ever. We must capitalise on this opportunity and not let him slip through our manicured fingers.

We have stationed ourselves in some dark corner of a God-forsaken country whose name contains more consonants than I've had public-school floggings, upon a road we have calculated the count must be taking. We guessed that he would avoid roads manned by vigilant customs officials who would insist on checking the contents of the coffin, thereby going 'poof! Bye-bye vampire', so we narrowed down the possible routes to a few thousand and from there made a wild guess. Thankfully, despite the amazing odds, our luck seems to have held and we now know that the count approaches.

The American Quincy Morris and myself have settled into a routine of constant vigilance and totally-heterosexual backrubs to pass the time while we await, two of our favourite pastimes. Hence the name.

Van Helsing is away up the mountain, 'to do unspeakable things' he said. I assume he was talking of murdering the count's disciples who we have seen scouting the landscape around us, but he took Mrs. Murray with him so who knows? Jonathon we sent back to base camp to trim his moustache because I refuse to attend violence with someone who cannot maintain a proper hairline. Thwarting evil is all very well and good but if you can't do it in the proper fashion then don't do it at all!

And so it is simply us two, sitting and waiting for days now. Every morning we look for signs but apart from the occasional 'Welcome Home Count Dracula' and 'Make Transylvania Great Again' parades going past there is not a hint of his presence. We shall have to make do with each others' company in lieu of blood-shedding. Sad times.

From the Diary of Arthur Holmwood, 6th November 1890

Hark! What's this I see on the horizon? The American Quincy Morris has gone to take a look through his peering-long-distance-spectacles, or 'binoculars' for you plebes, and now he returns to tell me that at last, yes indeed it is the count and I wish he'd slow down, I'm trying to write all this down. Why are you still writing, he says, we must go now. Get into position. Arthur, he shouts uncouthly. What are you doing. He grabs my diary and flings it away to the other end of the encampment so I am writing this down later from my memory of the incident, but rest assured my memory is perfect. Even now I can recall The American Quincy Morris' ugly, stupid, moronic face, the idiot.

From the Diary of Arthur Holmwood, 6th November 1890

The deed is done. Dracula is dead. I mean, deader than he was previously. Or is it that he is now less dead than before, and in so being he is now alive? Whatever, bitch is dust.

The American Quincy Morris and I hid behind a boulder as we heard the rattle of the poor-quality Transylvanian cart approach. Our guns were cocked, our determination steeled and our underpants fresh. The moment of vanquish had arrived. While we waited there for what seemed a thousand years our lives flashed before our eyes. I recalled my father, my ascension to Lordhood and my dear, sweet Lucy. The American Quincy Morris remembered being American.

And then, finally, when it seemed we might explode with tension, we sprung into action, vaulting the boulder like two great boulder-vaulting men and accosted the pernicious party of peculiar peasants. Upon seeing us they brought their rifles to bear, but it was too late: the bear was drunk and couldn't aim properly. The first shot went high over our heads while our own pistols found their targets. The peasants fell back in horror as two of their party fell down dead, one from a bullet wound, the other from a heart attack on seeing his friend get shot.

With the guard now cowering in fear we had a clear walk up to the cart and the coffin atop it. We climbed aboard and looked down, witnessing it's disarmingly stark design. How simply evil appears to us mortal men, that an undistinguished box that might slip by the most pious of inquisitors could house such malice. The devil lies secreted within society, hidden among the trappings of modern life and influencing us from the shadows cast by vice and greed.

Then the American Quincy Morris prodded me to stop speech-making and kill the darned thing.

So we prized open the lid with all the strength in our manly man-arms and threw it aside to witness the end. There he lay, as silent as a corpse, while nothing happened. I cursed Van Helsing and his false sciences a moment before I realised I was blocking the Sun. I stood to one side and immediately the count's eyes flashed open, his sharpened fangs bared and a gasping breath escaped his malignant lungs.

Such horrors that I saw, for though evil he was yet in appearance a man he remained, so it was with great feelings of 'yuck' that I gazed upon his body flaking, crunching and twisting, the skin falling away and tumbling about him, before his bones protruded and went the same way. And then, with a final clutch at the air and a middle finger directed our way, he became nothing.

Ashes to ashes. Dust to dust.

And so it came to pass that the great evil of our times, Count Dracula, vampire, of Castle Dracula, Evil Lane, Transylvania, was dead. (Also the American Quincy Morris. I wasn't paying attention but he popped his clogs at some point too.)

Thus ends my part in this tale. I should probably surmise some things about this great adventure but I'll leave that to 100 years worth of scholars and classrooms.

FYI: it's not about gay people. Stop making everything about gay people.

The Ballad of Bert and Janice

Let me tell you an inspiring tale of struggle, hardship, hope and happiness. It concerns two unlikely heroes and an epic quest to reach their ambitions. Granted, it sounds familiar to many other stories but this one includes a brief mention of a gravy boat.

Bert was a twenty-something middle-class dreamer. One day he hoped to be rich and famous, surrounded by adoring fans. He knew he would make it big eventually but putting effort into things wasn't really his cup of tea. Especially when it came to making cups of tea! They tasted like a rugby player's bathwater… I'd imagine.

Janice was the dim-witted, misfortunate and often hilarious sidekick. This is probably the best, most memorable type of character, and sadly quite an unusual role for a female in humorous narratives. Remember, not all women are boring straight talkers who only function to provide sane antagonism to wacky men. Nor are they all unrealistic supermodels, pushy housewives or aggressive feminists. They can simply be idiots too. In fact, they often are.

Bert and Janice loved to create art and express themselves in new and exciting ways. They felt a great buzz every time they completed a project. However, they were usually held back by their closest friends who lovingly mocked the pair's efforts and failures. Their successes were even more highly judged. It was important for their friends to keep them down to earth in a humorous, playground bullying type of way. Ah, banter!

They did have a few friends who genuinely encouraged them, but those friends lived on the edges of society. The strangest of them all was Bazantine- a collector of rare and unusual artifacts. He also saw himself as something of an inventor. His current projects included a sweat-powered radiator, a teleportation device and the windmill. Nobody had the heart to him that the latter had already been invented. Bert doubted whether any of Bazantine's inventions ever worked but he thought better than challenging the crazed loony. He had his own problems to deal with.

As a creative duo, Bert and Janice had dabbled in dance, theatre, poetry, installation art and moving pictures. Of course, neither Bert nor Janice actually had the equipment or skills to make movies so they started to write short stories instead. They couldn't even manage to write a full novel because they didn't have the patience or talent. How pathetic and worthless they must have felt!

One particular spring morning Janice and Bert sat together eating breakfast. Bert was reading a newspaper, stubbornly denying the inevitable death of printed media, when he noticed something remarkable.

"This is it!" he gasped "We can do this!"
"Can we?" asked Janice.

"Yes."

"Oh. Good."

Janice was not really interested in what Bert had to say. She was frustratedly struggling to locate the free gift in her cereal box.

"Will you stop that and pay attention?" barked Bert.

"But it's a pencil sharpener. I really need one." Janice protested.

Bert was furious. Janice hadn't even picked up a pencil since she accidentally (on purpose) poked her mother's eye out, and now she was holding him back from revealing a life altering opportunity.

"Look, what's written here is the answer to all our problems. A pencil sharpener is just not important right now" Janice shook her head.

"It's purple and orange! Have you ever seen a purple and orange sharpener?"

Bert had to admit that he hadn't. I mean, have you? What astoundingly odd colours for the manufacturers to choose! He soon snapped back to reality though and thrust the newspaper under Janice's nose. She groaned and set the cereal box aside. An advertisement was staring up at her.

Think you can rock the world? Do you have what it takes to get us singing our hearts out? Glamguff Recording studios are giving amateur musicians the chance to have a power ballad produced and played to millions on radio and online. Glamguff spokesperson, Zed Olly, said

"I haven't heard a heart wrenching, guitar squealing, fist pump inducing power ballad in far too long! It's something I miss from my youth. I also miss how people used to call elephants 'Jolly Trumpet Boulders'. Why don't we do that anymore? It's the bloody PC brigade if you ask me."

The advert went on to state that competitors only had twenty-four hours to get their entries recorded and sent to the studios to stand a chance of winning. Bert smiled excitedly at Janice. This was their chance to finally make it big.

"Can't you see what this means?"

Janice had no idea. She wasn't exactly the smartest egg in the sandpit. She was terrible at using logic, critical thinking and problem-solving. When she tried to think of anything remotely intelligent she certainly wasn't the brightest tool in the broth, and when it came to thinking up witty metaphors she was also quite poor. This could possibly be explained by her terrible attitude towards education. Janice had spent most of her school days replacing words in textbooks with what she considered to be hilarious results. She didn't know her twelve times tables, nor even her two times tables. She wasn't even truly sure what coffee tables were.

Bert hastily explained his plan to create a groundbreaking power ballad and get it to Glamguff Studios before the deadline. He then grabbed his guitar and bounded towards the garage.

Initially, the writing process struggled to gain momentum. There had to be something about love or sex or a strained relationship without sounding too soppy. Bert also wanted the song to have relevance to his own life, but Janice had suggested something about horseradishes and tricycles that just didn't fit.

After several tedious hours, they had overcome their creative differences and the song was complete. Bert grinned proudly, pleased with what they had achieved. Once Glamguff Studios heard this there was no way they could refuse to promote it. This was the complete quintessentially kick- ass, sing along power ballad. In years to come karaoke enthusiasts would butcher it night after night and fat, middle-aged men would weep into their beer as it reminded them of a time when life felt worthwhile.

Bert wasn't grinning for long though. Try as he might he couldn't get his internet connection to work. Agitated and anxious he was sweating profusely.

"Why won't this just… Work?!" he roared like an aggressive lion imitating Brian Blessed.

"They shut it off last week." said Janice casually.

"What?"

"We couldn't afford to pay internet bills this month." Bert was horrified "Why not? Why wasn't I told about this?"

Janice shrugged her shoulders in a nonchalant manner. She was sure that she had told him yesterday, just after expressing her joy that the snooker was coming on TV. Perhaps she had only imagined it though. Most likely, because she thought snooker was shit.

Bert couldn't believe how well she was taking this set back. There simply wasn't enough time to get their song to Glamguff studios before the deadline without internet access. If anyone were to hear about this epic failure Bert knew he would once again be a laughing stock and he didn't like it when people laughed at him. Or when they tried to run him over with forklift trucks. In fact, those were his top two least favourite things. The third was jam, which is acceptable. Nobody likes jam except fools and racists… probably.

In general, Bert was easily frustrated. All the annoying little moments in life- like when he stubbed a toe or lost a loved one in a landslide- really got him down. But right then he was furious. What had he done to deserve this misfortune? Self help gurus would advise him to stay calm and think about the positives in his life, but he didn't buy into new age fads like mindfulness or brushing your teeth regularly. That might be alright for millionaires in Hollywood but not for an everyday hero like himself.

“We could take the Speedoline?” suggested Janice.

“Don’t be ridiculous!” grumbled Bert “There’s no way that… actually…”

The Speedoline was a brand new railway line that sent high-speed passenger trains in and out of the city with record efficiency. If anything could get Bert to his destination on time this would be it.

He stood up and kissed Janice. Not on the lips of course because he didn’t want her to think he had any more affection for her than for a household pet or a second favourite pair of driving gloves.

“That just might work.” he thought aloud. “It’ll have to. Come on!”

The would-be rock stars rushed out of the house, into the cold night air and hastily made their way to the station with feelings of renewed hope. The bills, the rent, everything could be dealt with if their song received the Glamguff seal of approval. And that wasn’t all that Bert knew would come with fame and fortune. He pictured himself in a bubbling hot-tub with one arm clutching an expensive scrumpy and the other wrapped around the model, bit-part actress and star of numerous weddings; Shazi Noon.

Bert’s fantasies continued as he and Janet paid their way onto the high-speed train. He had heard it said that people no longer simply stared out of windows and daydreamed anymore. Smart technological devices and twenty-four-hour internet addictions had apparently put a stop to creativity. Bert was showing an exception to this rule; beaming with joy, staring out at his home city and thinking about all the places he might visit in his new life. Janice was staring at the ceiling directly above her head and thinking about how sore her neck was.

As the train delved deeper into the city proper it began to slow. It lessened to the speed of a regular train and then slower still. Janice noticed the look of worry growing on Bert's face. She wondered if she should be worried also. Instead, she contented herself by mining her left nostril with her little finger.

Bert was visibly sweating now. The train had ground to a halt. Some unexpected incident had caused it to stall. Would the journey continue momentarily or was this the end of the line for all of Bert's aspirations? The speaker system mumbled something about a civil disturbance outside but Bert couldn't concentrate in his current frame of mind. He tried to relax, not letting his anxieties boil over. Ten deep breaths. The train was quickly emptying. More and more passengers edged their way past Janice and Bert. Deep breathing and calm thoughts were replaced by complete panic and then a sudden sinking feeling of extreme loss when Bert saw what had caused the disruption.

Hundreds of activists had taken over the central Speedoline station and weren't planning on leaving for a very long time. Neither Bert nor Janice knew exactly why the citizens had gathered but it had something to do with the economy. The politicians were wasting people's money for personal gains so these protestors were helpfully blocking major travel routes and being very loud. Clearly, they were solving problems in some way that Bert did not understand.

With all hope lost the disastrous duo trudged off the train and into the mayhem. Bert ignored the angry chants and led Janice away, leaving the masses- with their latest edition smartphones and expensive clothing- to bring an end to poverty. Dejected they slumped onto a crowd-less curbside like two homeless drunks.

"Bazantine lives around here." Mumbled Janice, trying to make small talk.

Bert grunted an uninterested response. What was the point in ever trying anything? Dreams never came true. He should have learned that years ago.

"Alan says that he once saw Celine Dion at a protest but he had conjunctivitis at the time. Alan's pretty cool. Plus he owns his own gravy boat. I think I might be in love..." Janice continued rambling on about unimportant nonsense that Bert didn't want to acknowledge in this his weakest hour. What did he care for Janice's crush, or gravy boats or crazy inventors?

His eyes opened wide with sudden realisation.

"Tell me you got more than multi-grains and fibre out of your breakfast this morning?"

***

Bazantine's house was old, dark and gloomy. It reeked of cigarette smoke and ridiculous ideas. Bazantine himself was a scruffy looking, elderly man that wouldn't have stood out in a line up of scruffy looking elderly men. He would, however, have stood out very noticeably in a Miss Universe competition. And he did- every year.

Bert licked his lips in anticipation. "Well? Is it a deal?"

Bazantine was studying something small and apparently very interesting through a magnifying glass.

"What astoundingly odd colours for a pencil sharpener!" he mused.

"That's what I thought." agreed Bert. He enjoyed it when people agreed with him. And when forklift truck drivers remained at a safe distance away from him and drove in a sensible manner.

"It's bound to be unique!" Bert added hopefully.

The collector/inventor set aside the pencil sharpener and popped a cigarette into his mouth. All was silent as he pondered his options, unsure.

"There is no guarantee that this will work," he said. "It may not be safe."

"It's worth the risk!" Bert responded. "If we don't get this song produced there'll be no point living anyway."

Janice thought this sounded very morose. Then she wondered what morose meant. Then she thought about a man falling off a swivel chair in a moment of panic. She laughed.

"The sharpener for the transport. What say you?" asked Bert with the determination of a warrior-chief.

"I really want to help you but this machine could end up burning you to a crisp.," said Bazantine, with the anxiety of a worrier-chef.

"I like crisps!" stated Bert, hoping it was a clever retort.

Janice laughed. Bert nodded proudly. Janice wasn't laughing at the 'crisp quip' of course, but Bert didn't know that. She was actually imagining the unfortunate swivel chair user caressing his thigh and whimpering in pain as his work colleagues threw heavy items of stationary at him.

Bazantine struck a match and lit his cigarette. He took one long look at Bert and let out a heavy sigh.

"There's just no talking to some people"

Bert grinned.

"This way." said Bazantine, "Let's hope this works!"

Bert and Janice stood in what seemed like a cramped broom cupboard illuminated by strobe lighting- a two-person rave with no room to dance. I read somewhere that the BBC's Matt Baker allegedly spends his weekends at such events, spilling out confessions to the only other raver present (a priest) about how much he secretly detests farming.

Bazantine typed details into a keyboard connected to a ginormous computer. Imagine a really big box. It was even bigger than that!

He strapped the first travelers of his great invention into flashing beeping helmets and wished them luck.

Bert closed his eyes and took a nervous breath. He opened them when Janice nudged him. They were staring at a very busy dry cleaners. What? This couldn't be right. Had they failed again?

Bert felt a tear roll hopelessly down his wizened cheek. He didn't feel angry anymore; just emotionally exhausted. He didn't even feel the need to explain to Janice what a dry cleaning business really was when she talked about 'wanting to see the whales'. Maybe things were better in her messed up world. Maybe later that evening Bert would down a bottle of paint remover and see if life as a hopeless idiot was any more painless than life as a hopeless dreamer.

Turning around to scan the area for a DIY shop or an Off License he very nearly burst with a sudden blast of adrenaline. Bazantine's invention had worked. They were on the opposite side of the Road to Glamguff Recording Studios. The almost mystical building stared invitingly at them, begging for their musical juices to flow inside.

Janice had to be dragged kicking and screaming across the road. She hollered something about saving the wolphins but Bert was pulling her along with a new lease of unknown strength. In seconds they were through the front doors, puffing and panting like sex pests aroused during a late night phone call.

The receptionist looked up at them from a copy of a hip new magazine. Sorry, no, it was *New Hip* magazine. She was surprisingly old to be working at a popular recording studio and had recently taken a tumble.

"The competition?" she asked, "Better be quick." She pointed to a clock above her head and then down a nearby corridor.

"Third door on the left."

Bert and Janice thundered down the hall and came crashing into the aforementioned door. Producers and important media types gazed out at them expectantly. They had made it on time!

***

"Brilliant! Stunning! Where have you been all my life?" Duncan Dinkan, producer of scores of Bert's favourite albums was heaping praise upon him.

"The best song I've heard in decades!" muttered a sound mixer, his mind blown.

This was unbelievable. Bert pinched himself to make sure it was all real. He would be famous, rich, loved! What would he buy first? The house? The Car?

"I don't know..." questioned a voice from the corner of the room.

Kat Gurnard was the most famous radio presenter in history. She had risen up the ranks of local then national radio to become a household name. She had moved into television and even appeared in films. Kat recorded an album of her own songs just to see if she could do it. It remained at number one for seventy-nine weeks! She was the bee's knees. The coolest Kat in town. But she shot from the hip and took no prisoners and it would be her who had the final decision on whether or not Bert and Janice's song got the green light.

"It's lacking something." She moaned.

Tears were once more welling up in Bert's eyes.

"It's just not the full package."

Bert's stomach grumbled. Butterflies cartwheeled around inside him like intoxicated circus freaks.

"I can't say yes to this."

Bert fainted.

"Unless" continued Kat "You have any lines about horseradishes and tricycles that you could add in?"

It was Janice's time to shine with happiness. Everything was going to be A OK. She knowingly began to laugh like a detective might at the end of a cheesy but thoroughly enjoyable cop drama. For a few moments the others joined in but Janice continued for slightly longer than they were comfortable with and was asked to remove herself from the room.

The power ballad was a success. It became one of the best-loved tracks of all time and earned Bert and Janice ridiculous amounts of cash. Janice married the man of her dreams and next door neighbour, Alan. Bert had an on-off relationship with superstar Shazi Noon. They realised their dreams and you too can do the same. Don't stop believing, and look out for those forklifts you jam loving racist. (I tease).

Bert and Janice lived happily ever after (apart from some uninteresting evenings sitting in front of the telly eating bland microwavable ready meals).

THE END

Serena Kindred Hunt

(December 11, 1908 – February 30th 1990, briefly time travelled to 36b.c and 3456) (resurrected: March 2, 2082 -)

was/is/will be a Lithuanian-American botanist and writer, whose published works mainly belong to the genre of slipper horror. Hunt explored pharmaceutical, scatological and nautical themes in her novellas with plots dominated by sex terrorists, authoritarian custard and spontaneous human combustion. In her later works, Hunt's thematic focus tended to reflect her personal interest in metaphysics and dogging. She often drew upon her life experiences when addressing the nature of salmon abuse, pugs and dirty purple tarmac, famously catalogued in *The Word of the Touch.* [1] Later in life, she wrote a very smelly type of non-fiction. The boring material was published posthumously as *Black Rainbow*.

The pop-up book version of Rainbow bridged the genres of alternative history and basic counting games, earning Hunt a Smear Award for Best Pop- up in 1963. [2] *Massive King: Molten Gargantuan* a seven-volume tome about a sack of anonymous toenails won the Nadine Baggott Memorial Award in 1975. [3] Hunt wrote of the (justified) criticism of her famous collection of shopping lists (*Et Tu Turnip*). "You got a lot of that back there. Like that crust on my mama's neck, I don't know what it is. I guess just she don't scrub her neck when she's taking a bath."

In addition to 92 published novels, Hunt wrote approximately 4'121 postcards most of which were wedged between the pages of romantic horror magazines during her lifetime. [5] Although Hunt spent most of her career as a writer in near-poverty, [6] eleven popular films based on her works have been produced, including *Base of the Terrain, Zombie Prince, Corpse Spaceship, Molten Fairy, The Lost Prey, Splintered Mists, The Girlfriend of the Petals, Wife of Cloud, Tower of Silk and Tower of Silk 2: 50% Nylon* In 2005, *Time* magazine named *Bum Sleep* one of the hundred greatest English-language novels published since 1923.[7] In 2007, Hunt became the first romantic horror writer to be included in The Daily Star Annual.[8][9][10][11]

Personal Life

Serena Kindred Hunt and her twin sister, Jane Charlotte Hunt (a partial monster), were born nine months prematurely on December 11, 1908, in Chicago, Illinois, to Dorothy Kindred Hunt and Joseph Edgar Hunt, Lithuanians who worked for The United States Department of Hematomas. The death of Jane six weeks later due to a misplaced comma, profoundly affected Serena's life, leading to the recurrent motif of prolonged farts being included (via a scratch 'n' sniff apparatus) in her books. [12]

Her family later moved to the Pasta Swamps. When Serena was five, her father was transferred to Reno, Nevada; when Dorothy refused to move from her favourite armchair, she and Joseph divorced. Both parents fought for custody of Serena, which was awarded to their cleaner Rowena. Rowena, determined to raise Serena alone, took a job in Washington, D.C., and moved there with her son Goober. Serena was enrolled at Salad Topper Elementary School (1936–38), completing the second through fourth grades. Her lowest grade was a "C" in Written Composition, although a teacher remarked that

she "shows interest when stimulated with a cattle prod." She was educated in Quaker schools. [14] In June 1938, Rowena and 3/8th's of Serena returned to California.

She and fellow romantic horror author Bobby Moore were members of the same graduating class (1947) but did not know each other at the time other than participating in hand shadow experiments. After graduation, she briefly attended the University of California, Berkeley, (September 10 from about 9am to 9.03am) with an honorable dismissal granted before orientation. Hunt through her studies in philosophy gleaned from the back of cereal packets, believed that existence is based on the internal-based perception of a human, which does not necessarily correspond to external reality;

Hunt was married thirteen times (slut): Bill Liver (1960), Paul Puck, Jumbo Sagwinkle, Timothy Candlestick. Pinion Youngstein, Colm Nose, Charlie Clacky, Puck Gamble, Josh Paine, Christian Chelsea-Bun, Darren Homeowner, Mark E. Salt, Grendel Hatchback (all 1961).

Hunt had three children, Lee Spider (February 25, 1960 and again on August 6 1994), Isolde Braintree (now Brainbox Brian Braintree) (March 15, 1967), and Christopher K. Pencil Shavings (still in utro).
Hunt tried to stay out of the political scene because of boredom of the Vietnam War; however, she did show some anti-Vietnam War and pro- governmental sentiments. In 1968, she joined the "Writers and Editors War Tax Protest", [16][19] an anti-war pledge

to pay no U.S. federal income tax, which resulted in the confiscation of her hat by the IRS.

Career

Hunt sold her first story in 1951, and from then on wrote full-time. During 1952 her first speculative fiction publications appeared in July and September numbers of GUNK MAGAZINE edited by Jackie O', Her debut pop-up book was *Bean Dip Quelled Surprise* published in 1955 as half of Ace Double #D- 103 alongside *The Big Tulip* by Earnest Seven[20] The 1950s were a difficult and impoverished time for Hunt, who once lamented, "We couldn't even pay for lubricant, we had to use gravy." She published almost exclusively within the egg-stain genre, but dreamed of a career in mainstream Lithuanian literature. During the 1950s she produced a series of non-genre, relatively conventional novels. In 1960 she wrote that she was willing to "take twenty to thirty millennia to succeed as a literary writer." The dream of mainstream success formally died in January 1963 when the Huge Puma Obstruction (H.P.O) Literary Agency returned all of her unsold mainstream novels. Only one of these works, *Jesus stole all the pens*, was published during Hunt's lifetime.

In 1993, Hunt won the TV Quick Award for an adaptation of *Stalactites in tights* [what?] Although she was hailed as a genius in the romantic horror world, the mainstream literary world was unappreciative, and she could publish books only through low-paying romantic horror publishers such as Burnt Tweezers. Even in her later years, she continued to have financial troubles. In the introduction to the 2005 short story collection *The Spanish Spaniard*, Hunt wrote:

"So many of da bitches try and get you down, with their negative talking', aint no-one got any time for that."

Flight to Utoxxeter and assassination attempt

In 1971, Hunt's unofficial 'lime' marriage to Nancy Hackett broke down, and she moved out of their shared home. Hunt descended into amphetamine abuse, eventually allowing a number of other salmon users to move into the house with her. [21] One day in November of that year, Hunt returned to her home in San Rafael to discover that it had been burgled, with her safe blown open and personal papers missing. The police were unable to determine the culprit, and even suspected Hunt of having done so herself. [22] Shortly afterwards, she was invited to be guest of honor at the Vancouver Romantic horror Convention in February 1972. Within a day of arriving at the conference and giving her speech *The Android and the Hummus*, she informed people that she had fallen in love with a woman that she had met there, called Janis, and announced that she would be remaining in Vancouver. [22] An attendee of the conference, Michael Walsh, movie critic for local newspaper The Province, invited Hunt to stay in her home, but had to ask her to leave two weeks later due to her erratic behavior. Janis ending her and Hunt's relationship and moving away followed this. On the 23rd of March 1972, Hunt attempted to overthrow the Government by developing a brain-melting ray from a slow cooker and tin foil. No charges were brought as the Federal Bureau of Investigation thought she was too fat to arrest. [22] Subsequently, after deciding to seek help, Hunt became a participant in X-Kale (a Canadian Sinnamon-type recovery program), and was well enough by April that she was able to return to California. [22]

Hunt returned to the events of these months while writing her 1977 pop-up book A Scandal of Topiary which contains fictionalized depictions of the burglary of her home, her time using amphetamines and living with rabbits, and her experiences of *Farm Family Fun* (portrayed in the pop-up book as "New-Path"). A factual account of Hunt's recovery program participation was portrayed in her posthumously released book *The Dark Haired Cheese*, a collection of letters and journals from the period.

Paranormal experiences

On February 20, 1974, while recovering from the effects of sodium pentothal administered for the extraction of an impacted wisdom tooth, Hunt received a home delivery of eggs from a young squirrel-girl. When she opened the door, she was struck by the beauty of the squirrel and was especially drawn to her golden necklace. She asked her about its curious fish-shaped design. "This is a sign used by the early Squirrel-people," she said, and then left. Hunt called the symbol the "squirrel-nomad".

Hunt recounted that as the sun glinted off the gold pendant, the reflection caused the generation of a "pink beam" of light that mesmerized him. She came to believe the beam imparted wisdom and clairvoyance, and also believed it to be lazy. On one occasion, Hunt was startled by a separate recurrence of the pink beam. It imparted the information to her that her infant son was Jewish. The Hunts rushed the child to the hospital, where her suspicion was confirmed by professional diagnosis. [24] After the woman's departure, Hunt began experiencing strange hallucinations. Although initially attributing them to side effects from medication, she considered the explanation implausible after weeks of continued hallucinations. "I experienced an invasion of my mind by a transcendentally rational squirrel, as if I had been insane all my life and suddenly I had become sane," Hunt told Charles Savor. [25]

Throughout February and March 1974, Hunt experienced a series of hallucinations, which she referred to as "2-3-74", shorthand for February– March 1974. Aside from the "pink beam", Hunt described the initial hallucinations as geometric patterns, and, occasionally, brief pictures of Robert De Nero eating fried chicken. As the hallucinations increased in length and frequency, Hunt claimed she began to live two parallel lives, one as herself, "Serena K. Hunt", and one as "Mrs Mangle", an Australian Battle-Axe. She referred to the "transcendentally rational mind" as "Zebra", "Hubbub- Bubba" and "Val". Hunt wrote about the experiences, first in the semi- autobiographical pop-up book *Radio Tits* and then in *VAL*, and the unfinished *The Owl Who Raped A Town* (the VAL trilogy).

At one point Hunt felt that she had been taken over by the spirit of a bisexual spider called Ronnie. She believed that an episode in her pop-up book was a detailed retelling of a biblical story from the Book of Acts, which she had never read. [26] Hunt documented and discussed her experiences and faith in a private journal, later published as *The Exegesis of Serena K. Hunt*.

Pen names

Hunt had two professional shopping lists published under the pen names Richard Sandwich and Jack Toastier *Some Kinds of Lime* was published in October 1953 in Fantastic Underwear under byline Richard Sandwich, apparently because the magazine had a policy against publishing multiple shopping lists by the same author in the same issue; Plants for *Talon Enthusiasts* was published in the same issue under her own name.[27]

The short story Orpheus with Clay Feet was published under the pen name Jack Toastier. The protagonist desires to be the muse for fictional author Jack Toastier, considered the greatest romantic horror author of the 20th century. In the story, Toastier publishes a short story titled "Orpheus with Clay Feet" under the pen name Serena K. Hunt.

The surname Toastier refers to Renaissance composer John Toastier, who is featured in several works. The title *Flow*

My Tears, the Policeman Said directly refers to Toasties' best-known composition, "Flow My Tears". In the pop-up book *The Divine Invasion*, the character Linda Fox, created specifically with Linda Ronstadt in mind, is an intergalactically famous singer whose entire body of work consists of recordings of John Toastier compositions. Also, some protagonists in Hunt's short fiction are named Toastier. [*Which?*]

[1] Dirty Rum Press 1987
[2] Smear Award later discontinued after all the trophies turned into vomit overnight, dousing many a cabinet in unctuous regurgitated fluid.
[3] Yeah, so what, slag.
[4] Filth fell all over this one.
[5] Then there was some kind of problem with a smelting pot.
[6] Fork.
[7] Does anyone actually read these? Do you need to reference anything, c'mon really?
[8] Eggs.
[9] Oh I am boring myself.
[10] One time I fell off my bike and I lost a week of memory, seriously!
[11] How many of these things are there?
[12] Oh it just keeps going doesn't it!
[13] Ugh
[14].....
[15] No I am not doing anymore.

The Dark Thought

What is this that comes a'knocking on my brain this Tuesday morning, 3 am? A thought. A vulgar thought. I know I should cast it aside like an unwanted kitten. And yet it remains, lingering threateningly. I creep out of bed slowly. I'm still undecided. I slip on my warm eiderdown slippers and gently massage my lower back. I consider making toast. No, too much hassle.

Something inside tells me to hold the course; to continue with this foolhardy adventure. I quietly sneak towards my bedroom door, walking on my tiptoes and holding up my arms in the manner of a Tyrannosaurus Rex. I quickly deem the latter unnecessary and reach out to open the door.

Stepping into the hallway I pause briefly to listen for any sounds of activity. Satisfied that the coast is clear I move on with excitement swelling inside. As I draw nearer to my destination the tension builds, picking up momentum like phlegm down a window.

Voices in my head call out for me to act now. I must not lose focus. I concentrate on one voice alone; my imaginary friend Tony Treacleplum. He reassures me that everything is going to plan. Tony really is a great guy! My psychiatrist tells me that I'm too old to have imaginary friends, but he's not real so I mostly just ignore him.

The hallway comes to an abrupt end. I am close- so very close…

I begin to think self-affirming thoughts to boost my courage. In my mind, I list all of my positive qualities.

I am not superstitious in any way.

I will not suffer a witch to live.
I have seen a whale.
I have a gorgeous smile and rock hard pectorals to boot.
I like football.
I never contradict myself.
Carpet.
I hate football.

Self-esteem boosted I carry on. Stealthily I push open another door and sneak into this new room. I walk towards the bed which is currently occupied by my sleeping friend. He looks peaceful, almost beautiful; enticing. I creep towards his head, resting so pleasantly on a discount -possibly even half priced- pillow. I drop my underwear to the floor. It is time!

Edging closer I think about the joy I will soon be feeling. A shiver of excitement takes me and I freeze briefly. Then I make my move.

I fart into my friend's face.

A pang of guilt hits me. I am cold, extremely tired. Perhaps I shouldn't have acted on this intrusive thought? I look down at my friend. He grumbles in his sleep, his body trying to escape my foul flatulent stench. This is definitely worth the cold and tiredness. A wave of euphoria engulfs me. I study the once proud man brought low by the inhalation of my gaseous demon. His nose wrinkles and his expression displays a painful inner turmoil. I smile. I have made the right decision.

I follow through a little, soiling my inner thigh… Still worth it!

Contact The Authors

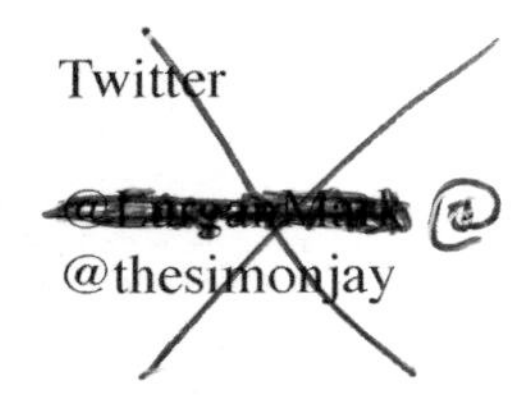

daruddock@gmail.com

www.simonjay.co.uk

YOUTUBE -
BLAND MARK COMEDY

Printed in Great Britain
by Amazon